The Music of Us

STILL LIFE WITH MEMORIES

VOLUME III

A Novel

USA Today
Bestselling Author

UVI POZNANSKY

The Music of Us©2015 Uvi Poznansky

This novel can be read as a standalone novel, as well as a part of *Still Life with Memories*, a series describing events in the life of a unique family from multiple points of view.

Published by Uviart
P.O. Box 3233 Santa Monica CA 90408
Blog: uviart.blogspot.com
Email: uvi.author@gmail.com

First Edition 2015
Printed in the United States of America
Book design, cover image and cover design
Uvi Poznansky

Contents

I Am Music

Chapter 1

Normally I recognize life-changing events only in retrospect. Not so tonight. Given what's just happened I know right away that this moment is critical. It would separate us, and the divide will grow, it will continue to widen beyond any hope of finding a way to bridge it.

I find it difficult to put it in words, to explain, even to myself, the significance of that phone conversation, of that one sentence, the one phrase I've hoped never to hear.

And I ask myself, Is this truly a surprise? Perhaps that word has been there for years, hissing persistently in my ear, waiting for me to accept it. All the while I pretended there was silence, nothing but silence until now, until this ring.

By nature I take my time realizing things. When I met Natasha, it took me a while to grasp the full meaning of being next to her, so close to her genius. I found the best part of who I was as I listened to the way she used to play the piano, the way she used to compose. Then, when our son was born, I didn't quite understand my role as a father, and even today I'm still learning.

He hates me now, hates me to the point of dropping out of high school simply to spite me. At the station this morning Ben looked anxiously at the bus as it arrived out of the mist. Meanwhile I remained sitting on the wet bench, hanging my head between my shoulders, looking at my fingernails. They looked blurry.

"Goodbye," he blurted, leaping to his feet. "I'm outa here."

Both of us knew he was headed nowhere and had no plans for his future, beyond a one-way flight ticket to Italy which he couldn't even afford. How he got it was a mystery to me.

"Don't go," I said, one more time.

To which he said, "I can't stay."

I tried to blink away the film of tears, which is where I saw the image of my own father, years ago. In a flash I remembered: he had been shrinking into the distance between this and that murky spot on the train window, left behind as I headed for a military induction center. I had thought I would come back one day with a measure of success that was not based on his advice. I had thought we would have time to mend the connection between us. Except for an exchange of letters, I saw him only one time after that. He had passed away a year later, which now brought to me the notion of my own mortality.

"Write to me, stay in touch," I told my son. "And take care of yourself."

I didn't think he heard me, but as the bus lurched, steering into the middle lane, Ben yelled something over the noise. I think he said, "Take care of Mom."

Watching the back tires splashing across a puddle as they turned the corner, I murmured, "I don't quite know how, son."

Back home I found Natasha sitting at her instrument with a vacant look on her face. In the background, the radio was making static noise, while capturing two stations at once with equal disregard to clarity. On one of them was a speech by President Nixon, calling the *silent majority* to join him and show solidarity with the Vietnam war effort, followed by some incoherent discussion among analysts trying to figure out what kind of majority it was and why, given its size, it remained silent until now.

On the other station was the song,

> What day it was I can't recall
>
> Time was so slow, down to a crawl
>
> All I could do was reach for you
>
> Or drown in dreams, so sad, so blue
>
> My arms open, just for you

I tried adjusting the dial, tried repositioning its antennae, and annoyed at myself for failing to get a clear sound of either one of the stations, I turned the radio off.

I considered asking Natasha to play something for me, but didn't. Instead I bent over the top of the piano, where the bust of Beethoven was perching, and touched my cheek to the cold reflection.

This time Natasha lifted her face to me. I plopped next to her on the bench and reached for her hand. Expecting no answer I said, "This place seems so empty, all of a sudden."

To my surprise she looked around and said, "So it does."

"He's gone."

"Who?"

"Ben."

"Oh," she said.

"I put him on the bus and waved goodbye to him."

At that, she fell silent. A moment later she whispered, "Don't I know how it feels."

"You do? Really?" I asked. "What is it, exactly, that you feel?"

She shrugged.

"Tell me, Natasha."

"You wouldn't understand it."

"Try me."

The phone started ringing just as she was about to tell me something. When I got up to answer, she waved her hand, which I understood, somehow, even without words.

Oh, never mind.

And as I lifted the receiver from its cradle I heard her mumbling something behind me, back in the living room. I held my breath, trying to catch the sound of her voice.

"Can't you tell?" she said, to no one in particular. "I feel loss."

For a moment I thought she was talking about our son, leaving us, or else about me, having an affair. Perhaps it made her stop calling me Lenny, which irked me. That, I thought, was why she treated me as a stranger.

"Is he blind?" She shook her head in disbelief. "Can't this man read my face? I feel as if I put my brain on a bus and waved goodbye to it."

Her doctor was on the other end of the line. He told me to schedule an appointment as soon as I can for an X-Ray for my wife.

"Hasn't she been through enough?" I asked, reluctantly. "So many exams, so many prescriptions, none of which has helped her so far. From one week to another I see her condition worsen."

"This time," he said, over my complaints, "it's a head X-ray."

"What for?"

"Just to rule out one particular thing."

"What kind of a thing?"

He hesitated, perhaps wanting to spare me some complicated medical term and the worries that come along with it.

So I persisted. "Tell me," I said. "What is it you wish to rule out?"

And he said, "Alzheimer's."

He cannot be right, can he? My wife is forty-five, much too young for anyone to connect her name with an affliction affecting the old. So I think about what he said for a few days, during which I do not schedule any appointments for her. Instead I just stay around her and try to focus on my writing, which is not easy because, just because. She is agitated at times, other times she is looking for her diary, and even if I place it right there in front of her, she cannot bring herself to write a single sentence, and even if she could, it's hard to decide which has become worse: her handwriting or her spelling.

"What is it, dear?" I ask. "Tell me."

"I just sat down at my piano and tried to buckle my seat belt."

"You must be tired, really tired," I say. "Go to bed."

In my heart I curse myself for being stuck in a rut, and curse her for pulling me down there in the first place. So to exact a little revenge on her I take the diary, after she has gone to the bedroom, and for the first time, without regard to her privacy, I open it.

I open it to the last legible page. It is dated exactly a year ago, and in it Natasha says:

Once I find my way back, my confusion will dissipate, somehow. I will sit down in front of my instrument, raise my hand, and let it hover, touching-not-touching the black and white keys. In turn they will start their dance, rising and sinking under my fingers. Music will come back, as it always does, flowing through my flesh, making my skin tingle. It will reverberate not only through my body but also through the air, glancing off every surface, making walls vanish, allowing my mind to soar.

Then I will stop asking myself, "Where am I," because the answer will present itself at once. This is home. This, my bench. The dent in its leather cushion has my shape. Here I am, at times turbulent, at times serene. I am ready to play. I am music.

But until then I am frightened, frightened to the point of panic. Even in my daze I sense the eyes of strangers. Their glances follow me down the street. Stumbling aimlessly from one place to another in the darkening city, turning around this street corner and that, I am amazed to realize that every building looks like an exact replica of the previous one. It baffles me, but I tell myself, with an increasingly shaky tone, that I am not lost. I cannot allow myself to think that I am. I will find my way, right after taking a deep breath to regain my calm. Then I will try to separate familiar lines out of this urban chaos.

Perhaps this intersection is not that far away from home. I am trying to map it in my mind, but the street signs are of no help, of course. Reading them has become such a chore lately, forcing me to traverse one garbled letter after another and connect them without forgetting the beginning of the word. I would like to believe that if street signs were written in notes I could play them in my mind. I could make some sense of them, because that is the language I understand. I am music.

The streetlamp next to the curb seems familiar, I think. So does the way electric light flickers inside, buzzing on and off, off and on. It strobes with a certain rhythm, as if trying to convey some coded message. I have heard this sequence before. It has a particular type of silence towards the end of it, which I sense quite vividly, but cannot explain in words.

The fear of finding myself lost is not a new feeling. It has been with me as long as I can remember, erupting now and again ever since I was a six-year-old girl. I never tell anyone about it, not even my husband, Lenny. Why? Because he seems to adore me not for my lips, which have lost their rosy shine in recent years, and not for my red hair, which has started to thin out, but for the magic I evoke, for the way I used to play, reciting complex, truly challenging pieces with barely a glance at the notes. He finds it inspiring.

My son, Benjamin, is in school. He knows the name of the street where we live and would be surprised to learn that every once in a while I forget it. I tend to forget the name of the city, too, so I ask him, and repeat what he says. It stays with me a while longer this way.

I never tell him about myself at his age, because it may open his eyes to see me, see who I am becoming. To him I must remain a mother. To my husband I must remain a woman. I keep the truth from both of them. No one in my family should guess that having lost my way, I am becoming a child.

This is the memory I withhold from them: at the end of my first day in school, I stood outside by the gate. I waited. I waited there a long time. No one came to pick me up. So I told myself that perhaps I could find the way by myself. I stepped out onto the street. It looked unfamiliar. By high noon, gone were the long tree shadows that used to point the direction back home. Hours later, after a frantic search, my father found me at the other end of town, wandering aimlessly along the Santa Monica beach.

Perhaps he expected to see an odd, bewildered look on my face. But no, I fixed my eyes at the sea melding into the sky. The only way to tell them apart was to note that it was creased, as if someone pulled a cloth across it. I took my shoes off, felt the wet sand, and listened to the yawn of the waves. I was happy.

So now, what can I do but what I did back then: try to trace my way back to where I started? As an adult I should be able to do it.

After all I have prepared myself. I have learned to pay attention to details. I study them up close, perhaps to the exclusion of seeing what is around them. I admire the beauty of things, the way they present themselves to your imagination when you really focus. I note how a chip of paint flakes off a door and swirls in a gale of wind or how the handle of the door reflects my image in reverse, distorting it over its curvature as I step side to side and back again. No

*one else would bother over such trifles, but I marvel
at them.*

Reading what Natasha wrote I suddenly recall the date, the
exact date she must have done it, because that was the first time
she got lost on her way to the grocery store, and a cop found her
five miles down the road in the opposite direction and brought
her back home. He told me that she could not tell him her
address, and boy is she lucky for his patience, and so am I, we
should both fall to our knees and give thanks to God, because it
was a major headache for him, I mean for the cop not for God,
to figure out where she lived by the few clues she managed,
somehow, to offer.

And even as this brings back such a sad milestone in our lives
I find myself amazed, as I read on, that Natasha could capture
the dialogue with him with such clarity:

*"D'you know where you're going, Miss?" a
policeman asks me.*

"No, not exactly," say I. "I think I'm lost."

"You know your address?"

"All I recall is how the gate looks, out in front."

He gives me a look.

"All right," he says at last. "Describe it."

*"One of the slats along the fence has been knocked
off its vertical position, and it is hung, somehow, by a
rusty nail, dangling from the horizontal slat in the
back," I tell him, doing my best to come up with a
complete description. "A crooked hinge is fastened to
it, which lets the gate sway, turning back and forth
with this sound, this harsh, repetitive sigh."*

He can't help rolling his eyes.

"Very well," he says, tersely. "That's a lot of help."

"It is?"

"Not exactly," he mutters, under his breath. "Now, try to recall: when you peek over the fence, is there a number up there, on the building?"

"There is," I say.

He cannot hide his relief. "Of course there is! So tell me, what is it?"

"I don't remember."

"Can you draw it for me, at least?"

I shake my head, No. "All I recall is that beyond the gate are the weeds, swishing left and right of the pathway."

"Weeds," he echoes, raising an eyebrow, which complicates things for him because it stops him from performing another repetition of what he has been doing so far, which is rolling his eyeballs.

"Yes," say I, "And after that, a diagonal shadow."

To which he throws his hands up in the air, "Diagonal shadow!" he mutters. "What did I expect! Naturally that's what I get, asking for a number!"

This diary, I now realize, is a precious, unintended gift she left me. If I go back far enough through its entries I can put her together again. I can resurrect the woman lost to me. Her ghost may then become more real to me than the closeness of her body.

I turn the page, and hear her voice rising from its rustle even as she tosses fitfully in her sleep, down there in our bedroom.

I avoid telling the cop that as I recall, the shadow is climbing up, ever so stealthily, into the apartment building, suggesting a hint of the stairs. And I avoid telling him that when you lift your eyes to the window, up above on the first floor, you can see that the embroidered flowers have faded in the sun, especially near the bottom edge of the curtain, where the fabric is straightening out of its folds.

This is where we live. This is safety. It is the place I must find.

And once I am there, I will sit at my white piano and give a little nod to the bust of Beethoven, which is always smiling to me. Then I will lift my hands over the keys, in wait for that perfect moment, when music comes.

I'll be Dreaming You

Chapter 2

I must hide the difficulty, with which Natasha is now coping, from our son, until I fully understand the nature of it. My wife agrees with me, in her own way. Even in her confusion, she keeps telling me that there is no need to cause him unnecessary alarm.

"Let him be," she says, and I am relieved to see the look in her eyes. This morning, it seems a bit more lucid than it has been for days, which gives me some hope.

"You're right. No need to burden him with worries," I say, trying to sound cheerful. "It's just us now."

"Yes," she says. "All we have to rely upon is each other."

For a minute I am unsure if it is us she is talking about. And just as I begin to trust that she is, Natasha gets up from the bed and steps in front of the mirror, turning her back to me.

Her fingers brush across the decorative woodcarvings along the side of the frame. "All we have to rely upon," she says again, facing herself, "is each other."

This is not the first time she notes her reflection as if it were another woman. It happened yesterday too, so I should not be all that surprised. To remind her of my presence I murmur, "I'll take care of you, Natasha. You can rely upon me, always."

And when she says nothing I add, "You look so lovely, dear."

"And so does she," says Natasha, pointing at the glass. "So pretty, isn't she?"

In place of an answer I rise up and put my arms around her slender waist. Gathering her to my chest I catch, by accident, the tired gaze of the man on the other side of the mirror. There is no glint in his eyes. He has a deep pleat in his forehead, which contorts his expression into an odd kind of anger, into defeat.

I don't want to look at him, don't want to see the wet trail running down his chin, dropping into her hair, finding its way around her ear, down the long lines of her neck. He wraps his hand around her throat, perhaps trying to help her wipe her neck dimple, where his tears stay awhile, glistening.

In a flash she takes a step forward, flailing about as if to defend herself.

"Come back to me, Natasha," I whisper.

Looking at me through the mirror she asks, "So? What about this woman? D'you like her?"

I turn her around to face me, simply to prevent her from talking to herself again.

"It's you I care for," I say, brushing my fingers through her unkempt hair. "Only you."

My son, Ben, has been gone for a month now, staying in some youth hostel in Rome. If I call him, if I stumble into revealing how scared I am that his mother is losing her mind, he may listen. He may heed my fears, grudgingly, and come back here, not even knowing how to offer his support to me. Should I ask for it?

The last thing I wish to do is lean on him for help. He is not strong enough, and whatever the problem may be with her, I can grit my teeth and handle it, somehow, all by myself. Besides, I pray for a spontaneous change in her. I mean, her memory may take a turn for the better just as quickly as it has deteriorated.

Given this hope I decide that for now I will not schedule the head X-Ray that her doctor recommended for her. I figure she has been through so much—so many checkups, so many exams to rule out depression, vitamin B deficiency, and a long list of other possible ailments, so many types of medications. And in the end, all these attempts to cure her, or at least to understand what she was going through, have been in vain.

Up to now, the results have failed to produce a conclusive diagnosis, and this new X-Ray will be no different, because from what I have read, Alzheimer's disease can be determined only through autopsy, by linking clinical measures with an examination of brain tissue. So this new medical hypothesis is just that: a hypothesis. One that cannot be proven; one that cannot go away. An ever-present threat.

Perhaps all she needs is rest. Time, I tell myself. I must give her time. Meanwhile I resolve to keep her condition secret from everyone, especially from my son.

Let him enjoy his time away from home, his independence.

Since his departure I called him only once, three weeks ago, and said little, except for blurting out the mundane, "How's Rome?"

"Great," he said vaguely, adding no particulars.

I could not help myself from asking. "So, what about your plans?"

"What about them?"

"D'you have any?"

"For now I have none," he admitted, and immediately changed the subject. "How's mom?"

"Fine."

"Is she?"

"She is," I lied, hoping that the sound of my voice would not betray the tensing of my muscles, the tightening of my jaws.

"Oh good," he said. "Really, really good."

There is only one thing more difficult than talking to Ben, and that is writing to him. Amazingly, having to conceal what his mother is going through makes every word—even on subjects unrelated to her—that much harder. I find myself oppressed by my own self-imposed discipline, the discipline of silence.

And what can I tell him, really? That I keep digging into the past, mining its moments, trying to piece them together this way and that, dusting off each memory of

Natasha, of how we were, the highs and lows of the music of us, to find out where the problem may have started?

To him, that may seem like an exercise in futility. For me, it is a necessary process of discovery, one that is as tormenting as it is delightful. If the dissonance in our life would fade away, so will the harmony.

Sometimes I go as far back as the moment we first met, when I was a soldier and she—a star, brilliant yet illusive. Natasha was a riddle to me then, and to this day, with all the changes she has gone through, she still is.

I often wonder: can we ever understand, truly understand each other—soldier and musician, man and woman, one heart and another? Will we ever again dance together to the same beat? Is there a point where we may still touch?

Unsure how to overcome the distance between my son and me, I wonder at the apparent ease with which my father seemed to communicate with me, starting at the time when I was drafted to the Army, nearly thirty years ago.

At the time, this ease surprised me, because back home, talking to the old man had become next to impossible. He had been growing hard of hearing and—even worse—refusing, in his own stubborn manner, to admit it.

"Can't you raise your voice?" he would ask. "Why d'you keep whispering like that? What's the matter, you afraid to speak out?"

And when I repeated my words, louder this time, he would respond by cupping his ear and blurting out at the top of his voice, "Eh?"

But then, once the conversation was transferred to paper, it started flowing. I found myself waiting eagerly for his letters and care packages, but would never admit it to him, which is something that today, I regret.

In 1940, the idea of the United States getting involved in WWII was unpopular, yet it became real overnight, when Congress passed the Selective Service Act. A year later, in October 1941, I became one of the lucky recruits. To me, it felt like an opportunity for adventure.

I boarded a Long Island train, and when it pulled with a whistle into the large brick station at the induction center, I was eager to begin my three months basic training. It was intensive: march, drill, read manuals, tend to your rifle. The instructor was all muscle, and the first thing he said was, "I'm your mother, father, and uncle, and you'd better respect me. Anybody who doesn't believe me, step out!"

I didn't believe him, but stayed in line. So did the others.

"The Marine Corps," he said, "is one of the most elite fighting forces in the world."

More or less in unison, we said, "Yes, sir."

"We serve on U.S. Navy ships, protect naval bases, guard U.S. embassies, and provide an ever-ready quick strike force. You know why?"

Not one of us dared to ask, "Why, sir?"

So he went on to say, "To protect U.S. interests anywhere in the world. That's your mission. And as for mine, you know what that is?"

"No, sir."

"To beat you into shape."

"Yes, Sir."

After that, we had to get our uniform tailored. Your blouse had to be form fitting and your pants should not be hanging. I was issued my new uniform and equipment, which made me wish, "If my dad could see me now!"

Meanwhile, my father rushed one care package after another to me. Looking now at the shoebox where I stored all of his letters, it's easy to figure out what connected them, what connected us.

Knowing my fascination with the stars, and especially with movie stars and with performers of both classical and popular music, he sent me a constant stream of news and magazine clippings. Among other things there was a tape of a song titled *I'll be Dreaming You*. Being bashful at the time, I had no girlfriend at the barracks, nor did I have one left behind—but even so, the lyrics evoked a painful longing as if I had one, as if I recalled the sweetness of her lips:

The magic of your kiss. your eyes

And now like then, the bells do ring

Was it the spell of sunrise

Or the scent of spring?

The fading tremor of the train

Who knows if we shall meet again

In another envelope, where the corners have frayed and the paper has browned in one crumpled spot and another, my father attached a carefully cut clipping from a Newsweek article, which announced, "Today, with Europe's musicians reaching for guns instead of violins and trumpets, with opera houses and concert halls dark in many foreign cities, the United States is expected to experience an even bigger music boom."

I remember writing back to him, asking for a photograph of the famous Wagnerian soprano of the Metropolitan Opera company, Lotte Lehmann, whose voice had fascinated me before she disappeared, for quite a while, from the airwaves. Before Germany annexed Austria in 1938, she had emigrated to the United States—only to be declared an enemy alien here. In my eyes, this injustice made her seem like a damsel in distress, which added to my infatuation with her.

Dad had little to tell me about Lotte, because apparently, the promised musical boom had to silence certain talents, talents that were not deemed American enough by those who orchestrate public opinion. Such, I learned, was the sacrifice demanded by patriotism in times of war.

Instead of the photograph I requested, which must have been difficult to find at the time, my father sent me a clipping from LIFE magazine, dated August 1941, showing a movie starlet named Rita Hayworth, whose hair I imagined as red despite the fact she was black-and-white.

Kneeling seductively on a soft bed, she wore a white, silky nightgown that hugged her slim waist and stretched over the roundness of her hips. The black lace trimming her low-cut top gave away the curves, the ample curves of her breasts. She must have taken a deep breath just before the shot, which made her cleavage more pronounced and her allure—ever more provocative.

And her eyes, oh, the sultry look in her eyes! It was directed just a bit over me and off to the side, making me wish she would turn and once, only once, bring me into view. I pinned her above my bed, so Rita may visit me in my dreams, and promptly forgot all about Lotte Lehmann.

Then came the day I unpinned Rita Hayworth and replaced her in my thoughts with another redhead, even though I had no photograph of her to hold close to my heart.

It all started with a misdirected shot.

The M1 Granad, with which our company was practicing shooting skills, is a semi-automatic, shoulder-fired rifle loaded by inserting a metal clip that contains eight rounds into the receiver. Once the eighth round has been shot, the empty clip automatically ejects with a notable noise, a ping that would cost the lives of many soldiers, as it would provide the enemy with a clue as to their whereabouts, especially in close-combat fighting.

That morning in training camp it was not the sound of loading, nor was it that distinct ping that alerted me to danger, but the whisper of blades of grass tearing asunder, falling with a whoosh left and right as the bullet came flying straight at me. Like a thunderbolt, it hit my shoulder. There is nothing friendly about so-called friendly fire. Searing pain started spreading to my arm, my entire quivering body. I staggered into a spin and fell onto the soft soil of the earth.

My mind drifted in and out of consciousness. At some point I felt a stretcher bouncing under me, and realized I was being carried somewhere, perhaps to the army hospital. I heard someone ask, "Is he still breathing?"

Wincing in pain I tried to answer, but my tongue would not move.

I recall hands, many hands touching me, grasping my arms and legs, lifting my body onto some hard surface. Then they started to apply direct pressure and elevate my limbs, perhaps to control the bleeding.

I passed out. I came to.

With the bullet isolated from the flesh and pulled out, splints and dressings were applied to immobilize the injured area, which was then wrapped with a dressing. I glanced at my left side. It was beginning to look like a mound of white gauze.

I got a glimpse of the sterile table next to me. It was littered with empty syringes, clamps, and a heap of cotton swabs, most of which were drenched in blood. And there, in their shadow, lay surgical Mosquito forceps. Normally they would be used for halting flow in small blood vessels, but right now they were holding something between their delicate, serrated tips. A bullet.

I passed out. I came to.

A couple of weeks later, one of my friends, who planned to apply to the Juilliard school upon completing his military service, came to my bedside to say goodbye, as he would be transferred the next day to a naval base in Pearl Harbor, Honolulu. At hearing this I cursed myself for my misfortune.

The injury robbed me of the opportunity to travel to an exotic place, to see the world. How could I prove myself, now?

"Get up," said Aaron. "Enough moping about. Tonight, we're going to celebrate!"

"Why?" I asked, sulking. "What is there for me to celebrate?"

He winked. "Jane Russell is coming in, to entertain the troops."

"Really?"

"Nope," he said. "And Betty Grable—"

"Yes? What about her?"

"She's not coming either."

"I get it. Next you'll be telling me about Rita Hayworth. She's staying out there in Hollywood, I bet."

"Yes, but," he said, "we do have a performance at the camp tonight—showgirls, musicians, a band, and what not! Quick, get up, get dressed! We're going to go see it!"

"Haven't you noticed? I'm injured," I said, pointing at the dressing that bulged over my shoulder. "This thing is huge, and so is the pain!"

"Enough," he said. "No more moping about."

"I won't be able to move my arm, let alone put it into the sleeve of my shirt."

"Your legs still work, don't they?"

"Yes, but—"

"No buts," he said. "Stand up!"

I leaned on him as he helped me into my russet-brown leather-soled service shoes. Having tied my laces

Aaron took off his olive drab cotton field jacket and wrapped it loosely over my shoulders. He tried to straighten the notched lapel collar, but the mound of gauze towering over my right side forced it into an odd shape.

"Oh well," he said, and gave a final pat over the buttoned shoulder loops.

I tried not to cry, "Ouch!"

"Relax," he said. "Lopsided is a good look for you. Seems muscular on one side, vulnerable on the other."

"Really?" said I, wishing for a moment that my father could see me now. After all, I needed someone to be proud of me—or, failing that, have pity on me in my weakened state.

"Really," said Aaron, in his most reassuring tone. "The girls at the show, they'll fall head over heels in love with you, especially that redhead kid."

"What redhead?"

In place of answering, he asked, "You like classical music, don't you?"

Which forced me to repeat, "What redhead?"

"Relax," he said. "Like I said, she's just a kid. But from what I hear, no one can match the way she plays the piano."

Moments later, before the nurse would come on her rounds to check my vital signs, I hobbled out of the hospital gate with my friend. The air was cold and it started forming into slaps, sharp slaps of wind. From afar, the outline of the auditorium, where the show was about to begin, seemed to hunch its shoulders under the weight of the clouds. The closer it came into view, the giddier I grew with excitement.

As a child of the depression era I could never afford going to a live show. With a meager allowance, frivolities were deemed too expensive, so the only glimpse I got of glamor up to now was from afar. How much more brilliant it would be when for the first time in my life I would witness the spotlights, feel the beat, and let my heart open to the passion of onstage performers!

I was especially amazed that a classical pianist would be selected for a show at a military center. Conductors, percussionists, and brass players had a decent shot at playing in a military band—but singers, string players, and pianists found themselves confronted, lately, with the question of how their talents might be used to benefit the Military. I figured that this kid must have been gifted at her craft, or else volunteered to take part in the show for free.

I had no idea what played in Aaron's mind when suddenly he asked, "You know how to tell that a girl is a virgin?"

Unsure what to say I shrugged, which was a mistake, because it made me feel my wound more sharply than before.

"Well," he demanded, "do you?"

"You tell me," I said at last.

"You know it by her neck."

"Really?"

"Really," he said. "Virgins have long necks. Always."

As an amateur artist Aaron must have gleaned this nugget of arguable wisdom from traditional oil paintings, where throughout the history of art virgin Mary is depicted with lovely, elongated lines as she cranes her head, doting on her baby.

Afraid to show my lack of experience in the matter of virginity I hesitated to ask what happens to those long necks at the moment of deflowering. I mean, did they automatically contract?

Between the two of us he was the expert, or so I thought. For sure I had a lot to learn from him. Too bad he was about to leave camp the very next day. I made a mental note to myself to pay more careful attention to women's necks from now on.

Meanwhile I said nothing. A light rain slanted into our path, and with every step forward, I prayed that my wound would remain dry, and the pain—bearable. All the while there was one tune that kept humming louder and louder in my head.

I'll be seeing you.

At first the song conjured the well-known black-and-white pinups: Rita Hayworth rising to greet me from a her luxurious satin sheets, Betty Grable in her bathing suit giving me an enticing over-the-shoulder glance, and Jane Russell, back against a haystack, inviting me to come in from the cold and find shelter in her shapely arms.

I stepped into a puddle and in a blink, a strange thing happened: these images receded, they swirled away into a gray blur, over which my mind formed an entirely new image: the pale face of a girl, a girl with red hair. I was enamored with Natasha even before laying eyes on her.

The lyrics suggested a past, they evoked a yearning for a future long before our first moment ever came to be.

I'll be dreaming you
In every path I'll find your traces
Going back to all our places
All night through

With a Light from Above

Chapter 3

The auditorium at Camp Upton could accommodate well over three thousand men, seated on benches to watch a boxing match or a movie—but tonight, for this show, there was barely any standing room. The door was slightly ajar. We stood outside of it, under the projection of the roof, over which the rain started to dance. Through its tapping, we listened to the sounds of marching bass drums coming from within. They were somewhat muffled, because of being cast back, like a whiff of second-hand smoke, over the shoulders of the GIs who crowded the place.

From the back, all of them looked identical, because their heads had been shaved according to the military regulation cut, using a straight razor with little effort to blend the border with the full head of hair above. My friend, Aaron, decided to lure them out of their place in line to move us forward. His plan was sure-fire: he pulled out his box of Chesterfields, lit one for himself, and used the second to tease the soldier waiting in line just ahead of us.

"Hey," he said. "Want a cigarette?"

"Sure," said the soldier.

"With us, it's Chesterfield," said Aaron, quoting the popular commercial slogan. "The cooler, better tasting, definitely milder cigarettes. Everywhere you go, they satisfy."

"Don't play with me," said the other. "I'm ready for it."

But Aaron was in no hurry to part with his coffin nail. Instead he took his time doing an imitation, a sexy imitation of the operatic singer, Risë Stevens, who had been featured recently in a three-color ad dressed as *Carmen*, holding a butt between her fingers.

Imitating her deliciously sultry voice, he uttered, "You might say I'm careful, that's why I say Chesterfields satisfy me."

"Satisfy yourself," muttered the other, in an exasperated tone.

"You don't want it all that bad, do you?"

"Hand it over, will you?"

At last, "Here, step this way," said Aaron, guiding him aside, in the direction of the mess-hall. There, he let him have his pleasure, after which he winked at me, hinting I should take the soldier's place in line.

They stood next to a pile of discarded things, which at first looked to me like pineapple fruit, glistening in the rain. A heartbeat later I realized what these must have been: faulty MK I grenades left over from old times, perhaps WWI, and no longer used for training, because of having been replaced, lately, by the MK II grenades.

With the ciggy between his lips, dangling this way and that, "Light me up," said the soldier.

Before I could say, "Aaron, for God's sake, don't!" Aaron did.

"Got your orders yet?" he asked.

To which the soldier replied, "Not yet. You?"

"Heading to Honolulu."

"Where's that?"

"Hawaii."

"When?"

"Tomorrow."

"I hear those Hula dancers are hot."

"Yes," said Aaron. "That's what everyone says."

Then he left the soldier to his puffs of smoke and came back to join me in line. And tapping the next shoulder, just ahead of us, "Hey! " he said. "Want a cigarette?"

It was then that I caught a low, intermittent noise, growling somewhere in the background. At first I thought that one of those metallic pineapples was not quite as faulty as expected, and might be ripening in a big hurry into an explosion, as a flying spark from that match might have lit its fuse—but no: there, behind the pile, a jeep nosed its way around the far corner of the building and then spun its tires into the mud, digging itself into to a full stop.

A short, stocky figure, wrapped up to her ears in fur, emerged from the driver side, narrowly avoiding landing in the sludge. Then the woman turned around to guide down another figure, who was too quick for her. Light-footed, the girl skipped over the puddle. Reflected in it I spotted her coat flapping open. In a flash it revealed a slender ankle and the bend of a knee.

I became so curious that without thinking twice I bolted out of my place in line, paying no attention to Aaron, who cried out from behind, "You devil, you! Hey, where d'you think you're going?"

And when he saw me following the two figures around the building, he called yet again, "Lenny, you'll lose your place in line! Come back! The back entry is for performers only!"

From the lightbulb above the door, yellow light poured down, painting the draped turban of the girl in silhouette, yet fleshing out the middle-aged woman in full detail.

Looking at that hairstyle of hers I thought it might serve as a domicile for a couple of birds, but could not imagine them staying there too long, as they might be asphyxiated from the buildup of daily dousing of hairspray, which was meant, I suppose, to keep every strand firmly in place despite any blow of wind that might chance her way. For further protection from the elements, she held her hands straight up, stretching a bunch of papers between them to shelter her bird-nest from the rain.

"Mamochka," said the girl. "My notes! They'll be ruined!"

"You don't really need them, Natasha, do you? You do play so well from memory."

Once the door slammed shut behind them I counted to ten before sneaking in. The corridor around the back of the stage was dark. I found my way by touch, guided by the blaring sound of saxophones, trumpets and trombones, under which I could detect a rhythm, composed of drums, bass, piano and guitar, pulsing a cord progression that gave reference for the rest of the band.

Suddenly I heard a whisper, which made me sink back a step or two into the shadows, in between two columns of stacked up benches. At this point I was still hoping to remain unnoticed.

There they stood, at the other end of the corridor, taking a peek at the stage. In a low voice the girl said, "Mama?"

The fat woman scratched the edge around her bird-nest, perhaps because all that hairspray—which became common recently, after the patent of the aerosol process—made her skin itch. Then she whispered back, in a heavy Russian accent, "Yes, Natasha?"

"Look," said the girl. "Isn't it amazing, the way these dancers shake everything they've got?"

The woman clicked her tongue. "What can I say but one word: Shame! Shame! Shame!"

"That's three words, mama!"

"Who's counting?"

"I am," said the girl. "Listen to the clapping! Everybody loves what they do! How do I follow an act such as this?"

I took a step or two closer. On the other side of her, seen through a curtain that covered the narrow opening, spotlights flooded the stage. Three female performers, dressed in khaki skirts and wearing black pumps, were doing their number: a hit song titled *Boogie Woogie Bugle Boy Of Company B*, which told the story of a bugler, a top man at his craft, who was reduced to blowing the morning wakeup call at camp, because the army could find no better use for him.

They sang the last verse swaying their hips with great flair, twirling their military-style neckties, and marching out directly into the audience. Then they invited cheering soldiers, one row after another, to join them in dancing their way back up the stage. When at last the performers waved goodbye, the entire place roared with applause.

"No one will want to listen to me," said the girl, in an anxious tone. "You know it."

"Listen, dear. Just do what you do best: play," said the other, instructing her daughter in the manner of a stage mom. Then, switching into the tone of a chaperone, she added, "Just remember this: pay no attention to any of them GIs down there, because God knows who they go to bed with."

"Mama!"

"Stick to one thing: notes, notes, and notes, and don't tell me it's three things, and don't count on anything I say, don't count it at all, not at all, not at all, because it's all only one thing, really. And above all, remember: don't look at any of them boys in uniform. Trust me dear, they're not for you!"

"Mama!"

The old woman opened her mouth to answer, but before she could utter another word, three things happened all at once: her eyes fell upon me, the girl clapped a hand over her heart, and the master of ceremonies could be heard behind them, stepping out to the center of the stage.

He bowed to the audience and cheerfully announced, "And now we take great pleasure to present the youngest star of our program, miss Natasha Horowitz!"

"Go, go, you go, girl," said her mama.

But to herself she mumbled, "Lordy Lord. Let's hope these GIs have some taste for something classical."

She reached over her daughter's forehead to adjust the feather in the little draped turban, which was whimsically designed by knotting together a couple of scarves. On other women, especially of the working class, such a hat would seem practical, as it was easy to create at home and kept the hair in place. On Natasha it added glamor. Impatient with all that fiddling over a feather, she removed it.

Out of the hat cascaded the most gorgeous, shoulder-length red hair, with a curl at the end of it, the tips of which were wet from the rain. The girl shook her head so as to let the drops fly out, slipped out of her coat and stepped out into the spotlight, without her notes.

Meanwhile, her mama turned upon me. She set her fisted hands firmly on her hips and took a big gulp of air, letting her breath expand inside her as if she were a balloon. Then she looked up at me trying to stare me down, as if I were the enemy.

"Who're you?" she asked, and without waiting for a reply she grumbled, "Go away! Go back!"

Up to that moment I had considered myself a fairly disciplined soldier, but the way she glared at me made me feel quite naughty, which on the flip side, compelled me to live up to a different reputation.

So feeling an urge, a sudden, irresistible urge not only to make an impression on the daughter but also to spite the mom, I slipped forward through the opening, and came onstage striding ahead of Natasha. Facing the audience I blew my cheeks, rather theatrically, into an imaginary bugle, which gained me a round of applause, as everyone thought my act must have been part of the show.

Then, with great flamboyance, I took the non-existent brass instrument out of my lips and clutched it to my heart, before making a spectacular leap offstage. While in flight, I totally forgot the injury I had suffered to my shoulder, only to be reminded of it, with a sharp shot of pain, upon landing. Stumbling onto someone's lap I tumbled further down onto the floor, from where I raised up my eyes to watch Natasha.

She came to stand at the edge of the stage, with a light from above focused upon her, which allowed me to see her clearly for the first time.

Her light-pink dress hung just below the knees. It hugged her figure, which was slim and straight like a pencil, with barely any curves. Under the squared shoulders, which were then in fashion, her scrawny arms hung by her sides as if she didn't know what to do with them, except for the long, delicate fingers that of their own, played in the air.

And oh, her face! Framed by the lovely chestnut curls, it was pale, and so were the freckles on her nose. This kid could be no older than fifteen. She was separated from the rest of us not only by the height of the stage and the radiance of the spotlight but also by the innocence in her eyes.

Having given us a nod Natasha turned to the Knabe piano and pulled the bench from it. Before sitting she smoothed the hem of the dress over her knees in the most prim manner. She lifted her hands dramatically over the keys.

Then—just as dramatically—she froze, as a collective sigh broke out when the master of ceremonies announced, "Tonight, folks, we're in for a treat. Listen to this piece: Rachmaninoff's Piano Concerto No. 3—"

"No!" said Natasha, all of a sudden.

"What?"

"You heard me," she told him, with a slight quiver in her voice. "I—I changed my mind!"

He glanced at her and then, overcoming a slight confusion, held the microphone to her lips.

"Before coming onstage," she said, "my mama told me not to look at the audience. But you know, she didn't tell me not to listen to them!"

Someone in the back clapped his hands. Others followed.

A rebellious smile started sparking in her eyes as she took hold of the microphone.

"So," she said, and her voice became strong and fully melodious. "I'm not going to play what I came here to play. Instead I'm going to give you something entirely different: a song that was written right here, in this camp, back in 1918."

Her mama must have fainted, because from the corridor, a loud thump was heard.

To divert attention from it, the master of ceremonies opened his arms to Natasha, muttering, "We, and the entire community of Yaphank, welcome you here—"

To which she said, "I find it interesting that it is home not only to Camp Upton, which is where we stand today embracing each other, but also to Camp Siegfried, a summer camp which teaches Nazi ideology."

He could not help asking, "Is that legal?"

"Protected by the 1st amendment, it is," she said. "Operated by the German American Bund, it is one of many such camps in the US since the 1930s."

Eager to change the subject, perhaps because he thought it politically explosive, he pleaded, "Tell us, Natasha, about the song you're about to play."

"It was composed by a friend of my late papa," she said. "He intended to include it in a military all-soldier musical called *Yip Yip Yaphank*, which for some reason never happened. He must have thought it too sad, too serious. It wasn't until two decades later, on Armistice Day, marking the anniversary of the end of WWI, that he revived it. Here is *God Bless America* by Irving Berlin!"

She handed the microphone back to him and turned to the piano.

I had heard others play the Knabe, which always sounds wonderful, as it represented the finest tradition of handmade, limited production piano crafting, which used the finest materials, from the tapered solid Canadian spruce soundboard to the premium German action and hammers—but no one brought it such sweet justice as when Natasha played it. She gave it a soul. From the very first notes, which started in the softest of murmurs, her performance gave me chills.

Since its introduction last year in a popular radio show, *God Bless America* had become not only a cultural sensation but also had been used as the official tune for the campaign of Franklin Delano Roosevelt. But here, in this auditorium, it turned into something larger and more meaningful than a popular hit or a political message. Her fingers awakened something in the belly of the instrument, in my guts, in the hearts of everyone present.

A prayer for peace.

For all these young men, who might soon be sent into battle, the song expressed unease over the approaching war. I was happy for my friend Aaron, who would be sent to a safe place, to Pearl Harbor, yet I did worry about the fate of the others, whose orders had not come in yet. All of us could sense those storm clouds, gathering far across the sea.

The Russian-born composer, Irving Berlin, was the son of a cantor who fled persecution in Europe. While he was growing up on the Lower East Side, his mother would indicate, time and again, that without this country her family would have had nowhere to go.

In 1940 the song was boycotted by the Ku Klux Klan, because they questioned both his right to evoke God and to call the United States his home sweet home.

In the face of such objections I found myself raising my voice, to pray, "God Bless America, land that I love." At first my voice was choked with tears, but then it cleared, as I sang, "Stand beside her, and guide her, thru the night with a light from above."

One by one, soldiers rose to their feet, many with tears flowing down their cheeks.

Meanwhile, the curtains behind the piano opened up to reveal all the performers of the previous numbers, holding hands. They swayed together, moved by the fears and hopes that this child evoked, by the powerful music that exploded from the keys under her fingers and hovered so divinely over us, sending pulse after pulse into our bodies, into our hearts.

Silence of the Muse

Chapter 4

I could not recall how I had made my way back to the hospital, nor did I have chance to say goodbye to Aaron, but the day after his departure for Honolulu I got a note, a mischievously cryptic note from him, telling me he had played a little prank on someone and used my name, but hoped I would forgive him for it, because what's a little joke between friends, and I shouldn't ask him any questions for now, because he wasn't prepared to answer, not yet, but I would soon find out, and not to be angry with him, because he had done it on a whim, and because he knew what I really wanted even if I didn't know it myself, and even if I did, I was too slow to admit it even to myself and too shy to act on it.

A week after my onstage stunt I was discharged from the hospital. My shoulder was still hurting, which made me unable to resume military training. Instead I was assigned to mess duty. It offered no glory, only heat, which turned my life into a sweaty existence. There I was, a lowly servant of his majesty, the cook, a man with chubby, greasy hands, whose pots kept spilling over, which provided an ever-present opportunity to order me about.

"Get up early in the morning, before the rest of the company," he instructed me. "Bring in the wood, start the fire, place food on the sideboard, replenish as needed, and when everyone is done, mop the floors, scrub the tables and then—"

"Then, can I eat?"

"Prepare the next meal."

The mess call had long died out by the time he allowed me to fill my mess-can and tin cup. Still, there were enough leftovers to showcase his dubious culinary skills:

Soupy, soupy, soupy, without a single bean

Coffee, coffee, coffee, without a speck of cream

Porky, porky, porky, without a streak of lean

By now most of my pals were gone. Some had gone onto guard duty or shipped to Camp Lejeune in North Carolina, where they would be put into infantry training. Others had been sent onto battleships. I imagined them in hostile terrains or in stormy seas, deployed to prove their courage in battle. They left families back home, and I envied them for bonds made, for love tested.

Meanwhile here I was, sweating to do nothing meaningful. There was no one with whom I could talk, except for the cook who expected me to listen.

Aaron was gone, too. I was curious as to the nature of his little prank, but how bad could that be? There was no choice but to wait and see.

I thought about him often, because before his departure he had given me a parting gift: his battery-powered Philco radio. I set it next to my bed and passed my hand over it with great awe. A Single piece of wood formed the top and sides, creating an arched shape that was not only practical for manufacturing but also delightfully beautiful. It looked like a cathedral. At night, when I returned to the nearly empty barracks, it helped my loneliness recede into the dark corners.

It was a sleepy, tranquil afternoon in Camp Upton on Sunday, December 7, 1941. There were only a few guys in the barracks. Each one of us was looking for a way to escape into his own dreams, in isolation from the others. Only the cook was heard, as he passed leisurely through the corridor with another guy.

"I'm not ready for our country to enter a war," he said.

To which the other said, "Even if we stay on the sidelines, we should prepare ourselves, don't you think?"

Bloated with pride, the cook answered, "I suppose you could call me a pacifist. I can't stand violence."

"What are you doing here, then?"

"I stick to what I do best: cooking."

"Your food," said the other, "is nothing to write home about."

"Well," said the cook, "it's an acquired taste."

"You think we're heading for war?"

"I hope not! I went through college during the thirties, when the emphasis was on the futility of war, and especially on the failure of the Great War, which is now called WWI, to settle any of the essential problems."

"You're right. They said it would save the world for democracy. It never did."

They parted ways. Soon after, sounds of a local broadcast of the Giants and Dodgers game on station WOR could be heard from one side of the building and at the same time, the regular CBS broadcast of *The World Today* could be heard from the other. Faint as they were, these sounds came from opposite sides to mix into each other, creating inscrutable echoes in the empty corridor.

The only way I could block away the noise was by listening to my favorite radio program, *The Chesterfield Hour,* which was sponsored by the Chesterfield tobacco company. For the most part, it featured big bands. But that afternoon, the announcer opened with, "Today, for a change, we have something quite unusual: a classical piece, one that has the reputation of being one of the most technically challenging piano concertos in the classical repertoire: Rachmaninoff's Piano Concerto No. 3."

At the sound of his words I leapt off my bed and turned the volume up, which made the cook grumble, "Turn the damn thing off, right now!"

He followed that with a few choice words, which had little effect on me. Outside the kitchen, outside his domain, I didn't care to play the slave, so I pretended not to hear a word of what he had to say.

Ever since that night when the redhead kid had entered my life—I mean, ever since she had decided, on a whim, to replace what she had intended to play with something else, something more suitable for GIs here, at Cape Upton—I had been growing curious to hear what I—what all of us—had missed.

The announcer went on to say, "Many experienced pianists dare not play this concerto. Some of them lament that they didn't learn it in their younger days, when they were still too fresh to know fear. Well, fear will not stop this performer."

By instinct I uttered her name even before he did. "Natasha Horowitz."

For many days I had been agonizing over the memory of how I met her, what a lousy impression I must have left in her mind by leaping off the stage. I kept asking myself, "How did you dare do it, what devil made you think you can share the spotlight with this girl, even for a single minute? Oh what a spectacle, what a sorry spectacle you made of yourself! What came over you?"

If, by some lucky, unforeseen twist of events, I were to find myself in her presence ever again, which I doubted, I would probably freeze, not knowing what to say. I was a nobody, and she—a star. Unreachable. Glamorous. There could be no connection between us, except through her music. It would illuminate my life and at the same time, deepen its shadows, giving full meaning to what I felt, in joy and in pain. Such is the power of a muse.

I leaned over the radio, eager to hear, ready to find delight in what she was bringing my way. I was hoping to grasp every note before the battery would run out of power and go dead.

It was then that my ear caught the first interruption. From a distant radio at one side of the building, a CBS anchorman broke in. At the beginning of the sentence his voice was still subtle, but by the end it became amplified into a blare.

"We interrupt this special news bulletin..."

Before I could cry, "Hey! You deaf? Lower the volume, down there," a second interruption occurred at the other side and a third one right here, out of Aaron's radio. In place of the music, which came to a strange halt after just a couple of notes, a deep, resonant voice said, "We interrupt," which was echoed once over, "We interrupt..."

Struggling not to become downright emotional, it trembled now on the airwaves from three different distances, to deliver the same grave message.

"The Japanese have attacked Pearl Harbor, Hawaii, by air. Details are not available. They will be, in a few minutes."

I caught my breath. The cook came running through the corridor, and several other guys gathered around him, all in shock.

"What did they say?"

"What do they mean?"

"Where is Pearl Harbor?"

"Should we do something?"

"Well, we're in it now," said the cook, and to my surprise he added, "We cannot let Japan get away with this."

"Let's whoop them," said one.

"Yes," said another. "Let's whoop them."

Meanwhile I was flipping stations on the radio, trying desperately to learn some details about what happened. The reports were vague, all except one. A reporter for KGU radio climbed to the roof of the Advertiser Building in downtown Honolulu, microphone in hand, and called the NBC Blue Network on the phone, with the first eyewitness account of the attack.

"This battle has been going on for nearly three hours... It's no joke, it's a real war," he said.

Then his voice was cut off.

My heart was racing—no, it was running the gauntlet of emotions, stricken by disbelief, confusion, fear, guilt, and most of all, profound sadness. I had never thought that anyone would dare attack the United States. Now I was wondering what was to come and how it would affect us, how this would affect America as we knew it.

I thought about the dead, and asked myself how many lives would be lost before this was all over.

Feeling lucky for staying behind, on safe ground, and at the same time blaming myself for it, I slapped my hands over my face and there, there was my friend, Aaron. He was, at this moment, on the other side of the world, but I felt his presence awakening in me, in the darkness of the palms of my hands. First he winked at me, as if to ask what's a little joke between friends, and

I shouldn't ask him any questions for now, because he wasn't prepared to answer, not yet.

Then he turned away from me, and in a snap, a strange thing began to happen: as if I came to be in his skin I shivered in fright, and saw it all through his eyes.

What I saw was a vision of the battleship where he was stationed, which was one of our eight battleships under attack. The USS Arizona, which used to be the symbol of our national might, of our naval dominance, was now engulfed in flames.

Falling into it through the black clouds of smoke was a bomb. It was coming with a shriek, and when it hit, for a split second there was no air.

Then sparks came raining down, all the way down through the hollowed floors. They hit the ammunition, then the gasoline, and soon the whole place caught on fire. The blaze roared with such maddening intensity in my head that I paid no attention to the silence, the sudden silence on Aaron's radio. Its battery must have run out of power. It was dead.

I stared at the surface of its wood, which arched into the shape of a cathedral, and prayed that I could still find a touch, a fingerprint, a remnant of Aaron's presence on it.

Sensing the smell of burning flesh I heard men crying out, I imagined them leaping overboard as the battleship exploded, as it was beginning to sink.

I caught the sound of demons screaming in my head and knew that this—this and no other—was the reason for the silence of my muse.

The Letter

Chapter 5

At long last, a change happened: I got my transfer orders to Camp Lejeune, a military training base in Jacksonville, North Carolina. So I packed my stuff and left Rita Hayward behind for the cook, who was delighted to pin her up between one failed recipe and another on the kitchen wall.

On the way to my new destination I learned what I could about it. Well over a year ago, a Major and his pilot had embarked on an aerial survey of both the Atlantic and Gulf coasts from Norfolk, Virginia to Corpus Christi, Texas. Then, circling over the Onslow County coast, they had seen below them fourteen miles of undeveloped beach, interrupted only by a single inlet. This would become an ideal area, they had thought, for maneuvering large formations, artillery firing, and the construction of a major base. One thing they had never taken under account was the local climate.

The thick pine forests surrounding the base, along with the dense underbrush and swamps, made it difficult for our troops to train and utterly unpleasant to inhabit, both of which ended up serving a purpose: they prepared us for later encounters. They toughened us.

But on the first day I was slow to grasp it and quick to complain.

"This camp," the officer told us, "is meant for amphibious assault training."

"Is it?" I wondered out loud.

"You have any doubts in what I tell you?" he asked, with a sudden twitch of his mustache.

"I do," said I.

And before I could hold back from digging myself further down into a hole I muttered, "I'm convinced that this place will shape a soldier out of me who'll be fit for nothing else but jungle warfare."

I was told to drop down at once and do a hundred pushups, which would not be all that hard if not for three things: I had to do them in mud, on my knuckles, and with his foot at my back.

That night, as tired as I was, I stayed awake for hours, not so much because of my aching muscles but because of feeling like a stranger in this place. I knew no one here. I did not belong. My heart was down at despair.

All I could do to keep myself from listening to the incessant crawling of snakes and buzzing of insects was turn on Aaron's radio. I thought I could find the music of my illusive star, the redhead pianist whom I had seen only once, and whose name—Natasha Horowitz— quickened the pulse of my heart.

Instead came the song, the popular hit song written just recently by Frank Loesser. It tried, somehow, to shape the ever-present feeling of foreboding about war into a snappy, happy beat.

"Praise The Lord1," sang the voice, "and pass the ammunition." And after three repetitions, to make sure everyone is marching in tune, at last came the promise, "And we'll all stay free."

I was not the only one to have trouble falling asleep. Down the hall, two other marines were wide-awake. They had come back from the movie theatre, the first one to be constructed in the camp, and were talking excitedly about nothing I cared about.

"Where d'you come from?" asked one.

"LA," said the other.

"Oh yeah? Did you ever meet a celebrity out there?"

"Not yet, but I figure it shouldn't be too hard."

"Really?"

"Really."

"How?"

"Simple! You get a manicure in Beverly Hills during the middle of the day."

"You sure? Is that when the stars come out?"

"They do, 'cause that's when real people are at work."

"Enough! No chatting, down there!" someone cried, and in the silence that followed you could sense tossing and turning, and later, murmurs and cries of men in their dreams. ·

---

1 "Praise the Lord and Pass the Ammunition was written by Frank Loesser and published as sheet music in 1942

A week after my arrival at Camp Lejeune, the heat and humidity were such that I longed for the good old days, I mean, the days of perspiration and exhaustion back in Cape Upton's mess hall.

It was on Christmas day that I got a letter, which had been mailed there and redirected to reach me here. At first glance I thought it must have been a mistake, which irked me to the point of discarding it, almost. No one but my father had ever written to me—but the penmanship could not have been his. My name was drawn in an unfamiliar, flowing calligraphic style. The envelope looked quite different from the ones he would send, and so did the stamps.

Dad would pay extra money to get the word *INSURED* printed prominently on the envelope in bold, capital letters. Invariably he would use stamps that featured famous Americans, each of whom was centered, rather formally, in a fancy, decorative portrait frame. I came to expect the usual lineup: a 2 cents stamp of Whistler, the artist, followed by a 2 cents stamp of Hopkins, an educator, a 2 cents stamp of Long, a scientist, a 2 cents stamp of Whittier, a poet, a 2 cent stamp of Cooper, an author, and a 2 cents stamp of Morse, an inventor. Forming a row at the top of the envelope, each one of these high and mighty characters seemed to have my father's eyes, which gave me a sense of trepidation, of fear to find myself a failure.

In a blink they might look down their noses at me and shake their heads ever so slightly, as if to say, "See? He's chosen us as for a reason, setting us as a model before you. Think, Lenny! Think what you're going to become! Plan your future! Do it now!"

But on this envelope, the postage was different. I used to collect stamps, and was surprised to see two identical, large, square ones that I had long wanted to get. Valued at 5 cents, they were posted one under the other, featuring the same image: a romantic drawing of a woman named Virginia Dare, whose life, according to popular folklore, was a mystery.

Having read about her I knew that her grandfather had returned to England in 1587 to seek fresh supplies and upon his return three years later, she had vanished without a trace. She was drawn holding a small bundle, which on second inspection looked like a baby. In the background was the pitched roof of a home. The image was lovely, but had no personal meaning, I thought, none at all. If not for the rarity of these stamps, I would have assumed that they must have been chosen completely at random. Even so, my curiosity awakened.

I flipped the envelope to its other side and thought I caught a whiff of perfume. I could not believe who the letter was from not only at first glance but also at the second and third, and had to rub my eyes to make sure I was not dreaming, not misreading the sender's name. Written in meticulous handwriting, there it was, her name and no other: Natasha Horowitz.

This, I thought, must have been someone's idea of a practical joke, but on the unlikely chance that it wasn't I decided to open the envelope with the utmost care. Hoping to insert some tool and rock it gently up and down till the glue gave way, I looked at the corner of the flap, searching for an opening, no matter how small. But no, there was none. The envelope was completely sealed.

I dampened a cotton swab and pressed it against one segment after another around the gummed flap, to soften the glue. Then, taking a deep breath, I lifted the edge. The paper came off intact, it did not tear, but it became soaked with water, especially where her address was written. Some of the ink began to bleed.

Thinking the address must be fake I neglected to blot it out. Instead I pulled out the letter and unfolded it, noting how unusually delicate it felt between my fingers. The first three words on it astounded me. They were, *Forgive me, Lenny.*

Up to this point I had been convinced that what lay before me was nothing but a farce and wondered how to discredit it, or failing that, how to play along with whoever contrived it, so as to regain control of this game and avoid making a fool of myself—but now I hesitated. After all, no one in his right mind could compose such a thing to pretend that it was a celebrity writing to an admiring nobody, a soldier. It was crazy, too crazy to be fiction. Therefore, this letter was genuine. Without a doubt, it was from Natasha.

How did she come to know my name? And why on earth was she asking my forgiveness?

Forgive me, Lenny, for not answering your letter right away.

At this I heard myself cry, What? I had written to Natasha? Why—when had I ever done such a thing? Not that it was such a bad idea, mind you! I wished I had thought of it in the first place, but apparently someone else had, and doing so he hadn't used his name, but mine.

Not knowing what he might have conveyed to her about me I had to gather every clue I could from what she wrote next:

I thought of explaining that mama hid your letter at the bottom of the stack of fan mail, assuming I would never get down to it, and that I found it only a few days ago, upon my return from the Catskills, where I had been on a long tour. While true, these are not the real reasons for the delay.

I'm not going to tell you the real reason because... Well, because I don't quite understand it myself. Besides, nowadays soldiers are being deployed to new places, so you may not even be in Camp Upton to receive this, and what I write here may never be read. I think I almost prefer it this way.

At reading this I asked myself, Who in Camp Upton could have pretended to be me, and at once the answer presented itself. Aaron! No one else but him knew of my infatuation with this girl. No one else would contact her on my behalf, which he did on the eve of being transferred to Pearl harbor.

In a blink I felt him step forth from a place far beyond, awakening in me, winking as if to ask what's a little joke between friends, and not to be angry with him because really, what's the worse that could happen, and he was simply tempted to use my name, it was for my own good, but I shouldn't ask him anything about it, because he couldn't explain things, not yet. Not ever.

In a strange way, the first three words she said could have been his. I heard his voice as a faint echo behind hers.

Forgive me, Lenny.

Then he faded, and she went on to say,

I was truly moved by what you wrote. It must have touched a nerve, yet I couldn't bring myself to reply, at least not immediately, and not in my safe, bland manner, I mean, the manner in which I thank all my other fans. Instead I had to gather my thoughts before putting pen to paper.

Do I remember you? Yes, I do.

I must admit: that night, when I first laid eyes on you, I could barely stop myself from giggling. I laughed not because you were handsome, and not because you seemed, at first glance, to be so hilariously funny, hopping all over the stage like a clown, marching behind me and in front of me and around me, but because you confused me. I found the closeness a bit sudden.

I suppose that to a stranger I may look like a regular teenager, someone who chats with her girlfriends and giggles a lot. I do, but don't let that mislead you. I feel utterly apart from them. My work is done in solitude—practicing my piece for hours on end, till I know it by heart, forward and backwards—but it's only when I face the crowd that I am reminded of my isolation. Even so, this is where I live and breathe. This is my joy.

I wondered, of course, why your right shoulder bulged to such a degree under that odd, unbuttoned shirt, but thought it a costume, meant to get a chuckle. I figured, like everyone else, that yours must have been part of the act, and had no idea you were suffering an injury. So thank you for mentioning it, which you did to remind me who you are, and which brought back something I had known about myself: the reason for painting a smile on the clown's face is to mask away any visible traces of pain.

You were performing that night and so was I, but not until holding your letter in my hands did I sense that perhaps, as you came to stand there beside me at an arm's length, for the duration of less than a second, just before you leapt off the edge, your loneliness was beginning to align itself with mine.

I'm revealing too much, too soon. At the same time I keep asking myself, Am I mad? Why am I doing this?

At reading this I wanted to tell her, I have no idea why you're making me so lucky as to hear you, hear your most intimate thoughts. Whatever the reason, keep doing it.

As if she heard me Natasha went on to say,

The safest thing for me would be not to mail this letter. Perhaps I should toss a coin in the air and let luck decide if it should be destroyed. Burning it to ashes will be such a relief. It will allow me to go on writing, simply to examine my thoughts in full light, in honesty. And then, poof! Let it all go up in flames!

I didn't question what your act meant that night. After all, I rarely question any of the strange things I encounter in show business. I rarely even pay attention to how I get to this or that recital hall. This may seem strange to you, because you expect my life to be full of glamor. But facing the spotlight, all these places seem a blur. Towns, streets, numbers...

Someone, usually Mama, drives me to where I need to be. Someone guides me to the stage and there, there is the piano. You wrote that you admire the way I play, but in truth music is the only thing for which I'm trained. It's the only thing I know.

And so, what seems perfect to you feels awkward to me.

You asked how old I am. I have just turned sixteen, Lenny. A sweet time, right? At least, this is what everyone says, but I don't feel it. Instead I sense a danger, still unformed, still somewhat vague, but already present here, inside of me, lurking underneath what is supposed to be a time of blossom.

The paper rustled between my fingers at the mention of danger. Even without knowing what she meant by that I could not help but care for her. I wanted to gather her into my arms and protect her, shield her from any and all threats, no matter if they were real or imagined.

The more she let me into her thoughts, the more I discovered how different she was from everyone I had known until then. To my surprise she had a moody outlook on life, a seriousness that was far beyond her years.

As if to prove me right Natasha added,

Being so different from other girls my age I often wonder about my future. My papa, who used to be a brilliant musician and a conductor, succumbed to Alzheimer's in the last years of his life, which makes me think... It makes me wonder.

If I ever lose my mind there will be no way for me to recover, as I don't have the skill to find my way.

So whoever seeks my friendship should consider this fault in me, because I depend on those closest to me, which may become a burden to you if we ever meet again, because you're unprepared for it.

Only when I lift my hands over the keys do I feel at home. Then I tell myself, I am here to sweep the audience away, let them take a wild leap with me into another sphere. And usually I believe this, even when it's hard, even in front of a yawning audience, some of whom seem to be in

dire need of sleep, or else in the grip of boredom. I
must believe in my purpose. I wish to inspire you.
   I am music.

Yes, I whispered. This is what you are.

At the bottom of the page, scribbled in smaller letters in
a somewhat hurried manner, perhaps because her mama
was calling her to dinner, was the last paragraph:

> *If I ever send this letter, and if you happen to*
> *get it, this is the one thing I want you to take*
> *away from it: I enjoyed your stories and would*
> *love to read more of them. Your words touched*
> *something in me, which is why I can't stop*
> *writing. But now I will.*
>   *And you, Lenny, you should become a writer.*

At reading the last sentence I could not help but sigh,
because it meant that from now on—should I be so
lucky as to engage her in conversation—I would have to
live up to a literary talent that did not even belong to me.

Even so, the next few weeks flew by in a delirium that by
day, tempted me to leap into the arms of the officer, twist
his mustache upwards, just for a change, and wet his cheeks
with kisses, with or without his permission, and by night,
made the crawling of snakes and the buzzing of insects
combine, magically, into a rhythm, an amazing rhythm that
could only be described as something entirely new to me:
happiness.

It was interrupted by one thing: the fear that if I reply,
Natasha might wonder about my handwriting. It looked

distinctly different than Aaron's. Should I admit that it was his hand that had written the first letter? Or else, should I report the healing of my shoulder, as a way to explain away the change in the slant of the letters and the smoothness of my pen-stroke?

Meanwhile I discovered that the style of my writing was the least of my problems. The one that was the most pressing was this: in my haste to read her letter I had neglected to blot out the wet spots. The ink on the envelope was, by now, quite smudged, having flowed from one stain into another and swirled all about.

I realized it would not be easy to decipher what had been written there. The only clear glyphs were her city and state, Summit, NJ. As far as I knew it was a far cry from LA, where by all accounts you could meet stars simply by getting a manicure in the middle of the day when real people are at work.

I cursed, cursed, cursed myself for messing up the one chance I was given to contact the girl of my dreams.

Then I figured out a solution of sorts. I created several copies of my reply and sent all of them to Natasha, each one to a different version of her address, according to a different guess, a different connection made while trying to find the pen marks down there, in the layer under this amorphous, inky puddle.

This was an exercise in uncertainty.

Would any one of these envelopes reach her? And if she would get them all, would she think me excessively obsessive with her? Would she deem my letters repetitive, even boring? Would she answer?

I braced myself for the wait.

Those Green Eyes

Chapter 6

E very evening, the officer would get back at me for the little
rebellious mishaps in my otherwise obedient behavior.
Ordering me to do pushups was no longer good enough for him.
Instead he opted to torture me by playing the same record,
which he had purchased some time ago, over and over again,
and preventing me from listening by talking loudly over it. It was
the English version of the Spanish song *Those Green Eyes*[2].

He was a stocky, middle-aged man with a pointy
mustache, who was bent on proving how well informed
he was on all things popular, and quick to tell me, in his
booming voice, that this song had been written back in
1931 but had not become a major success until now,
because what made it a hit was being performed by the
Jimmy Doresey orchestra and being made into a record,
which reached the Billboard charts on May 9, 1941 and
to this day it still held on to its number one rank,
because the bottom side of it was *Maria Elena*, which was
just as popular as the song on the top side, making it a
phenomenal double-sided hit.

---

2 "Those Green Eyes" written in Spanish under the title "Aquellos Ojos
Verdes" by Adolfo Utrera and Nilo Menéndez, 1929. The English translation
was made by Eddie Rivera and Eddie Woods in 1931.

While trying to block out his incessant flow of information, the lyrics stirred something inside of me, they brought to mind an image of a certain redhead, the twinkle in her bright, emerald eyes, which I had caught for barely a second, just before her Mama had stepped in-between us, back in Camp Upton, to wave me away.

I could just see those green eyes and felt the sadness they had left in my soul, because I knew she would never be close enough for me to kiss them.

After four weeks of listening to this song—just as I was beginning to give up hope, thinking that all the variations, the permutations of her address, to which I had mailed my letter, must have been not only convoluted but downright incorrect; just as I was beginning to accept that I would never, not ever, get another chance to be noticed by her, because as a star she must have had a million other admirers; and just as I was growing moody again, in a bigger way than ever before, cursing, cursing, cursing myself for being such a fool in love and in everything else and for having accidentally ruined her envelope, succeeding in nothing else but turning my good luck into a flop—the incredible happened.

Her letter arrived.

Unlike the first one, it was rather terse. Her tone seemed cold, as if to tell me not to bother about a reply. Was this really her intent? If so, why would she spend even one penny on an envelope, let alone on stamps, simply to tell me that?

In the first paragraph she said,

I got those letters from you, Lenny, all five of them, which is an odd thing in itself, and even more so considering they're all exact copies of each other. Perhaps you meant to approach five different girls, all of whom are named Natasha, and all of whom are in show business, and decided to save time by means of repetition, which makes me wonder. At any rate it seems excessive. And on the flip side, perhaps it's a good thing you said nothing, absolutely nothing about all the foolery I've written.

I've been too naive to share my thoughts with someone who's practically a stranger.

Having written to me at considerable length before Natasha must have been taken aback by the single sentence I had sent back—but really, for me there had been no other choice. I had to be careful with words. I had to use as little of them as possible.

I mean, what else could I have done in response to her praise, her heartfelt praise for my style of writing, when this so-called style was not even mine? It belonged to my best friend, Aaron, who without asking for my permission had done me a favor—or so he had thought, having the hutzpa to write to her on my behalf. I suppose he expected me to be grateful, which in my own way I was, to the point of grinding my teeth and swearing that if he wasn't already dead I would have killed him for that with my own hands.

On second thought I wished that his ghost would come back, that it could somehow be here to whisper in my ear, to hint at the secret of his fine way with words.

Months after he had perished in Pearl Harbor I would imagine, from time to time, that I could still sense his presence. So now, half-seriously, I begged him in my mind, "Teach me your craft—or at the very least tell me how to fake it."

I waited. I waited a long while. There was no sign, not the slightest clue. He answered with silence, to which I replied, "If you could use my name I wouldn't hesitate to write in your voice."

And for the last time I pleaded, "Don't leave me, Aaron. You've set the bar too high for me, so now she expects humor, anecdotes, and fine adventure stories. No one can do that better than you. How can I compete with a shadow of myself?"

There was no one to hear me, no one to answer. There I was, alone, utterly alone, staring at her letter, not knowing if she had responded to me or to him.

In the second paragraph, which was also the last, Natasha noted,

This time, your handwriting... Well, it's different, which I should've expected, because your shoulder injury, which I hope has completely healed by now, must have affected the way you handled the pen. Still, the contrast is quite stark. It shouldn't have surprised me, but somehow it did.

With that, she drew herself to a stop, and left her signature.

I wondered if Natasha suspected anything, if she guessed that it had not been my hand that had written to her the first time. From now on I should be even more cautious, because any ill-placed sentence, any superfluous word might betray that truth. Truth, for me, was the enemy. I figured I must make every effort to continue covering it up. And so I wrote back,

> *Please forgive the brevity. Life here in Camp Lejeune is incredibly tough, leaving me little time and little energy to compose something as beautiful as your first letter, which I must confess, touched me deeply. I said nothing, simply because I was still absorbing it.*
>
> *I had no inking what the life of a pianist must feel like, traveling to one place after another, and how you might respond to see the deterioration of a loved one. So sorry to hear about your papa.*

I considered signing off with, *"To you I am a stranger. Even so, this you must trust: I want to know you,"* but decided against it, for fear that it might seem too direct, too intimate, and worst of all, too simple, especially coming from a supposedly erudite man, a man who according to her must have been well-versed in bookish, exemplary expressions.

Below my signature I added an explanation, which at second glance looked a bit clunky, of how I had sent not just five but twenty-two exact copies of my letter, trying out different spellings of her street address, because her first envelope had accidentally become illegible, on account of being soaked with water, as a result of the extra care I took to lift the gummed flap without causing a tear.

To my amazement Natasha wrote back. She said that my explanation sounded unbelievable, so unbelievable in fact that she decided it must have been true, because who in his right mind would come up with an elaborate, tortuous excuse such as that.

And so we embarked on an exchange of letters, which started slowly. Then, over time, the intervals between one letter and the next grew shorter.

First she told me about changes affected by the war effort:

Mama read in the magazine: "Rationing has been introduced not to deprive you of your real needs, but to make more certain that you get your share of the country's goods, to get fair shares with everybody else. When the shops re-open you will be able to buy cloth, clothes, footwear and knitting wool only if you bring your food ration book with you. The shopkeeper will detach the required number of coupons from the unused page... You will have a total of 66 coupons to last you a year; so go sparingly. You can buy where you like and when you like without registering."

By Valentine's Day, her voice became warmer and a bit more confident. She began to trust me with little things, little stories about her life, stories that showed her to me not only as a pianist but as a sixteen-year-old kid.

She wrote,

Mama tells me to put on my roller skates and go to several neighborhood groceries because they've received a shipment of sugar, flour, butter or some

other rationed items, and she's given me some
ration coupons that can be redeemed for the
items. Every once in a while there may be Nylon
Stockings that Ma would want me to try to get. If I
can't find any, she might have to get them on the
black market.

I asked for her phone number. She gave it to me with a
warning, saying that she liked chatting with her friends for
long periods of time, so getting through to her would be
tough. It would be next to impossible.

This was true. After trying repeatedly to call her for three
hours straight I finally got tired of it and resorted to send
her a telegram, which I knew would be delivered at once by
a young man riding a bicycle in a Western Union uniform
and a cap, which is sure to get her attention. The telegram
said, "Get off the phone. I'm trying to call you."

Then I dialed again. It rang.

The Bell phone operator came on. I could hear her
fumbling about at the switchboard, which I imagined as
a high back panel, consisting of rows of front and back
keys, front and back lamps, and cords all about,
extending every which way, connecting the entire mess
into circuits.

At the other end, "Hello," said Natasha. Her voice
sounded intermittent.

"She said, Hello," said the operator.

"Oh, hi," said I.

"He said, Hi," said the operator.

We laughed. I could barely hear what I thought were
giggles, as they were breaking off, coming back on.

After a while the connection got better, but at the risk of it deteriorating again, we found ourselves talking rather fast.

I asked Natasha if she got my photograph, the one I had sent earlier that month. It showed me amongst others in a group of Marines, all of us dressed in uniforms, looking exactly alike.

She said yes, and was I the Marine second from the left, squatting, and in return I should expect a photograph of hers, which I'd better treat with extreme care, not the way I had treated her first envelope, which meant placing it in a dry, safe place, preferably close to my heart, because this is the earliest picture she had with her papa, so it was dear to her, and she's giving it to me as a special gift, and on an entirely different note, what would I say if she told me that this summer she plans to take some time off from performances, which would give us an opportunity to meet, and even if her Mama would object to this idea, because she protects her only daughter from dates with men, and with soldiers in particular, because in her opinion they're good-for-nothing low-lives who sleep who-knows-where with God-knows-who, she, Natasha, would love to see me if—and that's a big if—I could arrange a visit.

A Lowdown Groove

Chapter 7

Amazed by her invitation I knew that I had to see Natasha at once. I requested one week leave and did not hesitate to certify, as the form clearly instructed, that I had sufficient funds —which really, I didn't—to cover the cost of round trip travel and that I understood that should any portion of this leave, if approved, result in my taking more leave than I could earn on my unextended enlistment or current active duty obligation, my pay would be checked for such excess leave.

I was told that a leave would be extremely hard to get right now, because the Marine Corps was gearing up for a move. Even though the main battle would be in the Pacific, some of us, including me, would be assigned to serve with Navy units that operated in Europe. Starting in July I would be one of the Marines tasked to provide security for the American embassy in London. As part of this assignment I would meet with members of England's Royal Air Force. These meetings would lead into an exchange of information, and would have a significant effect, it was hoped, on the techniques and tactics developed for the use of Marine aviation in the near future.

Normally I would be looking forward to such an opportunity for travel, but not now, because it stood in the way of seeing my girl. After all. there would be an ocean between us. If not for the song on the radio, *I'm in a lowdown groove*[3], I would not have been able to find the words, the right words to express my mood.

"Oh," I sighed. "What a lowdown groove."

I was just about to call Natasha and tell her that I could not possibly make it when the officer summoned me to the office.

Rising from his desk, "I hear you want to go visit your girlfriend," he grumbled.

How he knew the purpose behind my request for vacation I had no idea. Word must have spread around, perhaps due to all those letters traveling back and forth between Natasha and me from one end of the country to another.

Snapping to attention I said, "Yes, sir, I do."

"Haven't you heard?" He huffed, puffing out his mustache. "We're at war."

"Yes, sir."

"War demands a sacrifice from all of us."

"Yes sir, it sure does."

"But for you," he said, acidly, "vacation would be a nice thing, wouldn't it."

"It sure would."

"A full week is out of the question."

Before I could stop myself I blurted out, "It is?"

---

[3] I'm in a Lowdown Groove written by Jordan Roy

He raised an eyebrow. "Even three days," he said, "would be next to impossible for me to approve."

I thought of asking, "Will you, sir?" But this time, luckily, I bit my tongue. Then I said, "I'd give my right arm to see her."

To which he said, "I suppose you're a lefty."

I was, but did not want to give him the satisfaction of confirming it, so I said nothing.

The officer went back to his desk and began sharpening the tip of his pencil. Then he crossed out the number 7 from 'how many days' and replaced it, to my surprise, with the number 3. Bending over his desk, he picked up one of the rubber stamps, rolled it for the longest time all over a pad of ink, and without uttering another word, pressed it against the paper. I had to hold myself from leaping forward to hug him, because there it was, rustling in his hand in bright, capital letters, the magic word: APPROVED.

Taking under account the travel time from Jacksonville, North Carolina, to her city in New Jersey and back, a leave of three days would allow me only a few hours with Natasha. That did not worry me at all, what did was an entirely different matter: I could not afford the round-trip train ticket, so had to make do with a one-way one.

Even worse, I could come up with no better plan of return other than hitchhiking, which meant that I might not be able to make it back to camp on time and could be punished severely for it, because as a matter of U.S. military laws, desertion was not measured by time away from the unit but rather by something more subjective, such as unauthorized leave with a determined intent to not return.

For now I put it out of my mind and boarded the train, focusing on one thing: getting to Summit.

Glowing in the bright morning sun, the city sat atop the Second Watchhung Mountain, one of the two most prominent ridges known as First Watchung Mountain and Second Watchung Mountain, both of them stretching for over forty miles. Summit was known to be an affluent place. Its people were rich and did not shy away from demanding what they wanted. Back in 1898, they had entered into a dispute over wires and telephone poles with the New York and New Jersey Telephone Company, a dispute which had been resolved by the edge of a knife. The city had acted. Wires and cables had been sliced off.

As I climbed up Broad Street, which was wider and straighter than most streets around here, a trolley stopped by and a thin, tall man with a slight stoop hopped out. Holding a clarinet case under his arm, he adjusted his Fedora hat, which was made of light woven straws with a center crease that was angled to the back. Taking one glance at me under its brim, he set the case down, tapped his feet, and threw his arms wide apart.

"Lenny?" he cried. "What a surprise! Is it really you? Boy, you've grown so much since I saw you last! Coming to visit your old Uncle Shmeel, are you now? Why didn't you tell me you're coming?"

"Well, I," I mumbled, as he gathered me into his arms. "I really didn't, I mean, I didn't know—"

"Ah," said Uncle Shmeel. His smile revealed a glint in his gold tooth, which was devilishly matched by the glint in his eye. "I see: too many years have passed! You've forgotten all about me!"

"No—"

"What d'you mean? No, you didn't know—or no, you did forget? I used to play my clarinet for you, one song after another, when you were ten years old, remember that?"

I did, but only vaguely. With a notoriety as a ladies man, he was not really my uncle but a distant relative, the great grandson of my father's great grandfather on his mother's side, or something like that.

"Good to see you," I said. "I hope all's well?"

"Now that," he said, "is a long story."

And without stopping for a breath he proceeded to complain that the introduction of talkies—which had started with *The Jazz Singer* in 1927, and had been followed, wouldn't you know it, by the Great Depression —that introduction had been devastating to many musicians, including him, why? Because he had come to rely on earning a living at the cinema houses, where silent films would be featured to the sound of live music, which would not only contribute to the atmosphere but also give the audience vital emotional cues, without which they could make no sense of the action.

So now if not for old Pearl, his girlfriend for the last ten years or so, who was incredibly generous to him on account of waiting for a marriage proposal, he would find himself living out on the streets, God forbid, or else having to play in Jewish weddings as a *Kleismer*, which in Yiddish meant the instrument of song, but thank God she adored him, which she did for no better reason than his improvisational flourishes, which in the past he had used to great advantage, earning not only his pay but also his reputation for virtuosity, which expressed itself in his manner of embellishing the drama onscreen, especially during scenes of horseback chases, so that even when special effects had not been indicated in the score, he would find a way to add galloping horses, which was not an easy sound effect to achieve, especially with a clarinet.

At last he gasped for air, which was my chance to take leave of him. I extended my arm to him, offering a handshake. "I wish I could hear some more," I said. "But really, now I must go."

"Why?" asked Uncle Shmeel, as he clasped my hand. "Are you late for a date?"

"No—"

"Then stay a minute," he said. "What's the big hurry?"

He took his hat off and I could see that he looked a bit like my dad, with his grey hair combed carefully backwards over a balding spot. And just the way things were with my father, there was no saying no to Uncle Shmeel.

"Look at you," he went on to say, astonishment ringing in his voice. "What a fine young man you've become! Look at the polish of your golden buttons and buckles, the mirror of your shoe, the white of your belt, so tight around that slender waist of yours! Oh, what a splendid sight! A marine: fit, trim, dashing!"

At hearing this I could not help but blush, because the way I chose to dress on this particular day was due, I admit, to nothing else but vanity. I wanted to impress Natasha.

"At first," I told him, "I considered wearing civilian clothes, but to my dismay forgot to bring my best pants, so instead I wore my dress blues, which were furnished to me at camp as part of my sea bag issue. This uniform has been worn, with few changes, in essentially its current form since the 19th century."

"By you?"

"No!"

"Of course not," said Uncle Shmeel. "What was I thinking? Unlike me, you weren't born back then. Would you believe it, I've turned fifty just a few weeks ago! I don't believe it myself!"

"Really?" I said, even though he looked his age. "Hard to believe!"

He flashed a big smile. "So now, tell me the truth. What's the uniform for? Some kind of a parade?"

I hesitated to answer, which was when he wagged his finger at me. "I knew it!"

"Knew what?"

"Don't you play games with me now! Someone should tell Walter Winchell, the newspaper and radio gossip commentator, so he can spread the news all over town!"

"I'm sure I don't know what you mean—"

"All of this," he said, pointing at me, top to bottom, "is because of a girl!"

"That," I said, "is something I can't deny."

"Of course you can't! Now tell me everything, will you?"

"What shall I say?"

"Where does she live?"

"Ten blocks from here," I said. "She's young, very young, and fiercely guarded by her Mama, who's extremely cautious about the idea of her daughter dating enlisted men."

"Which means that at the sight of this uniform, she'll flip."

"I'm afraid she will."

"Or else, she'll find you irresistible."

"That I doubt."

We stopped at the corner of an intersection, and I dashed into a flower shop to buy a bouquet of roses, even though I had little money left.

"I know what I can do for you," said Uncle Shmeel, now with a resolute tone, which made me hold my breath. I was hoping he might offer me some money, which was badly needed. I could use it for taking

Natasha out on the town and for the train ticket back to camp.

"This is your lucky day," he said. "The girl is going to embrace you and so will her Mama!"

And I asked, "She will?"

And he said, "Yes! You'll arrive at her place in style, which means driving my new car! At the sight of it, the whole neighborhood will be astounded, because money talks, even if it has nothing important to say, because its vocabulary is limited to a single word, success, and trust me, nothing says success better than a 1941 Ford Super Deluxe Convertible."

I was speechless, utterly speechless, to the point of neglecting to thank him, which to my relief, he understood.

"Now," he said, "about the car—"

"I'm not sure I can drive it," I said, hoping it didn't sound strange to him.

After the stock market crash of October 1929, which had sent Wall Street into panic and wiped out millions of investors, my father had lost all his savings. Since then he could not afford giving me money for driving lessons, let alone buying a car, both of which were out of reach for us. We used public buses, trolleys, and trains.

This year I had been trained to use a Harley-Davidson motorcycle. The military needed vehicles that were capable of quick handling and evasive riding. I found great pleasure in its olive drab-green color, its design, even its rattling noise, which exuded the masculine and rough-and-tumble essence. But other than the bike, and having driven a jeep once or twice around camp, I had little experience as a driver.

"Not sure you can drive it?" said Uncle Shmeel. "Just try, what's the worse that can happen?"

An answer wasn't expected, so I did not waste time looking for one. Instead I asked, "Are you sure?"

"Sure I'm sure!"

"Can you afford it?"

"No," he said, "but how could I say no to such a fine vehicle? I got it as a birthday gift. Pearl is grateful, so grateful to me for letting her cling to the hope that she can change me, despite all evidence to the contrary. She knows how to treat someone like me, someone who appreciates the more elegant things in life."

"You," I said, "are a lucky man."

To which he shrugged. "She's a patient woman."

Out of his pocket came the car keys, jingling.

"Here," he said. "You're going to have great fun driving her. She's such a beauty!"

"You mean, Pearl?"

"No! The car."

"That," I said, "was my second guess."

"She's sitting there idly," he said, pointing farther ahead, across the intersection. "There in the driveway, see? And she's doing nothing but trying to tempt me morning, noon, and night to take her out for a spin, which is the first thing I'll do as soon as I get my driving license."

"What's stopping you?"

"I keep failing the damn test."

We turned the corner and there she was, looking quite substantial in her wide, matronly body, radiating heat in the mid-morning sun. She was graced by the ample roundness of the front and rear fenders, which were shaped as puffed-out cheeks. The grille was a three-part affair with a tall center that nosed its way down in-between twin nostrils, low down on the fenders. I imagined that she knew I was coming for her.

As I turned the key in the ignition I saw Uncle Shmeel in the rear view mirror, taking the clarinet out of its case and putting it to his lips. Then, growing smaller and smaller as I drove away to Natasha, he could still be heard across the distance, blowing a tune for me. One note after another rose trembling in the air, awakening a mood, a joy turned into something inexplicable, into sadness, over which I murmured, "I don't need a song to prove that I'm in such a lowdown groove."

Memory is a Liar

Chapter 8

The last stretch of road, as I drove over the hilltop and turned downhill, was steep. Then, her house came into view. I recognized it from a photograph she had sent me. And yet, it looked somewhat different, less glamorous than I had expected. Unlike other houses in the neighborhood, it seemed to suffer from neglect. The roof seemed to be in dire need of repair, as did the wooden fence in front.

I had never driven this car before, and rarely have I driven any other car, except for the Jeep at the camp. So it took some effort to slow it down. Meanwhile I noticed there was someone at her doorstep: a milkman. Having delivered fresh milk in a set of glass bottles, he straightened up and looked at me in sheer astonishment. This, I figured, was not because of knowing that the car belonged to Uncle Shmeel and not because of knowing that it was a gift from old Pearl, who was incredibly generous to him—I mean to Uncle Shmeel, not to the milkman—on account of waiting for his long-overdue marriage proposal.

This astonishment was not even because the 1941 Ford Super Deluxe Convertible was known to have such a fine class distinction—but simply because it trumpeted like a disreputable, vulgar boor. The noise was such an embarrassment! Passing wind to mitigate the flatulent effect of beans would have sounded heavenly, by comparison. What was I doing wrong?

And another thing: What if I could find nothing to say to Natasha? After all, the last time I had met her was last year. When was that? October? November?

Since then we had exchanged quite a number of letters, but now, with the paper between us removed, there was something utterly frightening in having to face her and—even worse—to talk.

Oh, I could not forgive myself for neglecting to think of some topic, some lines to recite, should the conversation suddenly run dry.

Just my luck! It was too late to prepare myself now, because two things happened at once: first, I spotted the slender outline of a girl up there in the window, combing her long, red hair. And second, the front door opened, letting out her Mama.

Somehow I managed to bring the car to a stop. She took one look at me and with menace in her eyes, set her hands on her hips.

I fumbled to pull up the brakes. "Hello," I said.

And she muttered, "Not you again."

The woman was wearing a square-shouldered jacket, in the style that became popular recently, which also featured narrow hips and skirts that ended just below the knee. With so many men leaving for military service, magazines and pattern companies advised women on how to remake their suits into smart outfits. The alteration idea must have appealed to Mrs. Horowitz, because her husband, the famous conductor Benjamin Horowitz, had passed away only a few months ago, and the cloth would otherwise sit unused. Looking rather substantial in it, she plodded heavily forward, overtaking the milkman and heading in my direction.

I turned off the ignition and leapt dashingly out of the open-air convertible, which was the moment her expression changed. I could tell, by the way her jaw fell open, that the impression I made—or rather, the impression the vehicle made—was the best I could possibly hope for.

"Mrs. Horowitz," I said. "How are you this fine morning?"

To which she said, "It's already noon."

I went around the car to the passenger side and from there, took out the bouquet I had bought earlier. Red roses.

Opposite me Mrs. Horowitz leaned over the driver-side door, perhaps to examine the plush leather interior. It was then, in the face of her curiosity, that a question suddenly occurred to me. I asked myself, did I—or did I not—turn the front wheels towards the curb, to make sure the car won't roll?

And before I could make up my mind either way, I heard a low rumble as something gave way. The brakes must have become disengaged, which sent the car rolling downhill, letting a single red petal fly out of the passenger seat and swirl into the air.

I took a step back. So did Mrs. Horowitz.

She gasped. So did I.

Stumped by not knowing what to do with the bouquet I was holding, I shoved it into her arms.

"For Natasha," I said, and took off running after the car.

Luckily there was no traffic at the moment. The convertible sailed without incident along the middle of the road until reaching a horse-drawn wagon, at which point I braced myself for a crash. But the horse saw it coming and moved sideways, clearing the way. Had it been a car instead of an animal the story would have ended quite differently.

Now I thanked God that the only noise I could hear was not that of a collision but rather the huffing and puffing of the milkman who, having chased me chasing the car, arrived at his wagon and steadied it to stop the glass bottles from rattling inside.

I never imagined I could gain enough speed to overtake a runaway car. Somehow, I caught its door and held it with all my might, and felt it slowing, slowing, slowing straight into a ditch.

And now, standing there by its side, I had all the time in the world to catch my breath, and to agonize over the multitude of questions that started racing through my mind. Is the car broken? Should I try to drive it out of where it was stuck? And what should I tell Uncle Shmeel? How can I make it up to him?

Also, should I turn back to Natasha's house, even though her Mama was sure to point out the door? I was tempted to go there, especially because this time I had no need to prepare a topic of conversation, no need to sound smart, for one reason: the way I made my entrance into the neighborhood was all everyone would be eager to talk about, even Natasha.

It was then that I heard something, the whoosh of roller skates coming down the road in my direction. And as I turned, the incredible happened. Gliding with grace, there she was, coming at me with her hair glowing red, blowing backwards in the wind. Before either one of us knew what was happening Natasha ended up tripping on a loose stone, flying straight into my arms.

That moment I sensed the same rhythm, the same beat pounding in her chest and mine, which convinced me of one thing: despite messing up a 1941 Ford Super Deluxe Convertible, or maybe because of it, I was—without a doubt—the luckiest man alive!

But unfortunately, as moments often go, this one did not last. By instinct I drew closer and touched my lips to her forehead, taking in the fragrance of her hair, which must have been a mistake, I mean, not the fragrance but the thought of a kiss. Natasha pulled herself back from me, perhaps embarrassed because of the sudden, unintended touch.

With delicate, almost transparent fingers she straightened her skirt and smoothed an unruly curl that slinked down the left side of her face. She tucked it carefully behind her ear, slowly composing herself.

Then, catching her breath, "Now you've really done it," she said.

And I asked, "Done what?"

She answered by asking, "Didn't you read what I wrote to you?"

"What?"

"I said, you must make a good impression on Mama, must behave yourself this time, because she remembers you, and she does so not exactly in a good way, if you know what I mean, and to make matters worse she's suspicious of all men in uniform, because according to her they're here one day and gone the next."

I shrugged, and Natasha went on. "She says that nothing of value can come out of spending my time with any of them, because I'm too naive, and should avoid those good-for-nothing bums, because all they want is to take advantage of me."

"Sorry," said I. "I never got that letter."

"Would it have made any difference if you did?"

"Probably not."

"From now on, because of you, Mama's going to give me an earful, much more than she already does, each and every time I happen to bring up your name."

"Really? Like what?"

"She's going to repeat, over and over, 'He's not for you and I told you so,' until she's blue in the face."

"In that case you're going to have no choice but to fall in love with me," I said.

To which she said, "What?"

And I said, "With this much force, she's practically pushing you into my arms, isn't she?"

"I don't wish to rebel against her," said Natasha, under her breath. "But yes, she makes me so angry inside, she does."

"I should really thank her for it."

"Why?"

"If not for her I would be slow to sense this heat in you."

She blushed and fell silent for a long time.

Meanwhile I made myself busy looking at the front of the car. It was scratched, even dented in one place, but the front wheels sat on a firm surface, which suggested to me that with the right moves I could drive it, somehow, out of the ditch. I hopped into the driver's seat and steered the car gently till it climbed into the side of the road.

Watching me she said, a bit shyly, "You look different than I remember you."

"So do you."

"Really?" she said, her eyes glinting with curiosity. "How so?"

I held myself back from telling her that the first time, several months ago, she had looked like a kid, but not so anymore. Now her arms were no longer scrawny, nor did her legs look like pencils. She was still thin, but in a much more shapely way. Somehow I could sense the fullness of her breast, heaving rapidly under the pink blouse.

"Oh," I said, as I leaned over to open the passenger-side door for her. "There is a change in you, a subtle change, which I find hard to define even for myself.

Perhaps I'm imagining it, who knows. Memory can play tricks on you."

"It sure does," she said. "Memory is such a liar."

I laid my arm behind her, hoping she would lean her head against my shoulder. She did.

Then, as I started turning the vehicle to drive her back home, I heard her saying, mostly to herself, "But then, when you lose it, you lose your grip on reality. I've seen it happen. Long ago Papa used to teach me various memorization techniques, even for the most complex, most challenging piano music, but then, in his last days, he didn't even remember my name. He didn't know who I was. I'll never forget it."

Tears sparkled in her eyes. To spare her feelings I pretended not to hear.

In a blink she turned to me. "You won't understand what I'm going to say, because you weren't here to see, to witness what Mama and I went through during his illness."

"Try me."

"No," she said. "There's too much agony, even now."

"Let me hear it."

"Memory is a liar," she said, once again, "but even if it's not telling the truth I must hold on to it."

And a minute later she added, "I mustn't lose it or I'll lose myself."

It was a strange thing to say, especially on a first date.

"What happened to your Pa," I said, "will never happen to you."

"Is that a promise?" she asked.

I replied with a smile, finding myself dumbfounded not only by her question but also by the contradictions in her, the frequent change of mood, the stark contrast between her bright appearance and the dark soul that lived in her. It must have given depth to the way she played music, as it allowed her to soar with happiness and plunge into despair.

She wiped a tear from the corner of her eye. I wanted to hug her, to protect her, even from herself. But a little voice in me, sounding a lot like my father, whispered that I should get far away from her as fast as I could, because being so complex, she's bound to be trouble. I should find me a simpler girl, one with no worries in the world.

Natasha was right. I could not understand her. Instead I looked away. Then, in a flash, I had an odd premonition. I saw her in my mind, years later, fighting to hold on to the memory of her Papa, of her grief for him, and of this very moment, and little by little losing the battle.

And now, talking to herself again, she said, "He didn't remember my name. Thinking of how brilliant he used to be I felt such pain. I still do. I can only hope never to forget it."

Bei Mir Bistu Shein

Chapter 9

The girl opened the door and called out, "Mama?"

We heard the clap, clap, clap sound of slippers as Mrs. Horowitz came down the stairs. Having removed her square-shouldered jacket, the woman looked rumpled. Her brown shirt hung limply over a hunched back, and the front was equally ill tailored. It drew attention to the way her breasts dangled down, which reminded me of rumpled balloons with the air gone out of them, bouncing against each other as they hover in midair the day after a party is over.

Mrs. Horowitz stomped over and looked me in the eye. I thought she would say something about the car rolling downhill, or ask if it got damaged, but all she said instead was, "You again?"

I said not a thing and smiled at her as charmingly as I knew how, which must have done something to disarm her, at least for a moment. She let me in and asked Natasha to make coffee for our dear guest and a cup of tea for her, and on second thought no, not tea but hot, boiling hot water with a heaping teaspoon of honey, and on second thought no, just half a teaspoon, and not to forget, a squeeze of lemon, too.

I took a step over the threshold. The living room was huge, and the furniture—highly decorative, giving you the impression that you were transported, somehow, around the other side of the world and back in time, to a palace built in the second half of the eighteenth century in Russia. Every piece was gilded in a variety of hues: red-gold, green-gold, even silver. Here and there, some of the gold leaf was damaged, but that did not detract from the richness of the decor.

I was especially overwhelmed by the eclectic combinations of ornamental motifs. There were carved garlands of flowers and foliage, rosettes, shells, urns, harps, even sphinxes.

And yet there was something about the place that made it look not only in disrepair but also about to be deserted.

It felt—oh, how would I put it in words?—as if it didn't belong to this family anymore, as if they had stopped caring for it, for some reason. The floor was covered with dust. The iron chandelier hanging above the staircase had half of its light bulbs missing.

Opposite me a large window brought in a strange, hazy sight: the modern skyline of Manhatten, which looked utterly out of place here. The old curtains that framed it were badly frayed at the hem. The only thing in the room that looked intact was the piano, in which you could see a mirrored, upside-down view of faraway skyscrapers. They seemed to be plunging down into the polished, black surface.

Over the mantle hung three formal family pictures. When Natasha came back from the kitchen I asked her about them.

At once, her Mama cut in. "My daughter comes from a long line of musicians," she said, in her heavy Russian accent.

"Mama," said the girl. "I can speak for myself."

I pointed at the first picture. "Who's this?"

"This," said Natasha, "Is my great grandfather, the famous Abraham Horowitz, who graduated from the Kiev Conservatory at the turn of the century. He rose to stardom rapidly and toured from Moscow to Rostov-on-the-Don, where he was often paid with bread, butter and chocolate, rather than money, because these were tough times."

"And this?"

"This is Joseph Horowitz, my grandfather. He aspired to become a violin player, but his hand was damaged for life, when the riffraff attacked him during a pogrom in Odessa. So instead he became a music teacher. Later, he developed a method, a unique method to memorize long passages of music, by practicing the notes back to front."

"And this," she said, reaching up to touch the third picture, "this is my Papa, Benjamin Horowitz. When he came to the states he became a conductor. Meanwhile he took that method one step further. Instead of the traditional way of playing through the passage repeatedly, you would commit it to memory, or rather to your subconscious mind, by means of performing it every night before falling asleep—without holding the instrument in your hands."

"A spendthrift, that's what he was," Mrs. Horowitz blurted out all of a sudden.

"Now, Mama, don't start!" said the girl.

"Who's starting?" the older woman threw her hands in the air. "I'm already in the middle of talking!"

"Then please, please stop—"

"What, I'm not allowed to tell the truth? The only inheritance your Pa left us is a dream, the dream of you becoming famous one day, and oh yes, how could I forget, also a bunch of heavy loans on the house, without any means of paying them off."

"Why complain so much, Mama? It was fun for you, wasn't it, while it lasted—"

"Which wasn't too long, the way he gambled away his money! By the time his illness started, we were already hopelessly in debt."

"Mama!"

Undeterred, Mrs. Horowitz shook her head, which in turn shook her bird-nest style hairdo. "Years earlier," she said, "before he asked me to marry him, everyone was so, so very impressed with his talent. They predicted such a bright future for him. Where are all of them now?"

"But Mama," said the girl, "what does the bright future he had in the past have to do with the present?"

"It has everything to do with here and now. You," said Mrs. Horowitz, turning upon me, "yes, I'm talking to you! What's your idea of the future? What are you planning to make of yourself, young man?"

This question, I'm afraid, touched on a sensitive nerve. My father had pressed hard on me to achieve his dream: becoming a lawyer. Naturally there was no saying no to him. So before graduating from high school I had told him that I had registered at the university and would be majoring in Law, according to his wishes —but somehow I had neglected to mention that the closest I had ever come to registering was flipping through an outdated course catalog, while sitting on the toilet and dreaming about something else.

Being drafted the next year was a lucky thing. It had saved me from having to admit to him that I had lied. I had looked forward to military service. Not only had it promised travel, fun, and adventure but also relieved me of the old man's constant nagging.

So, what was I planning to make of myself? That was the question I thought I had escaped answering—until now.

I glanced at Natasha, hoping she can, somehow, get me out of this uneasy spot in the interrogation, but all I could spot in her eyes was a flash of curiosity. She, too, wanted to hear what I might say. I recalled her first letter, in which she had written, "*I enjoyed your stories and would love to read more of them. Your words touched something in me... You, Lenny, you should become a writer.*"

Well, I thought, how hard can that be? And expecting to make an impression on both of them I said, "I'm going to be a writer."

"No, really," said Mrs. Horowitz.

"Really!"

"Have you even been published?"

"No—"

"Of course not. Have you written anything worth reading?

"Well, not yet, but—"

"You interested in drama? Comedy? Some other genre?"

On a whim I said, "Drama."

"Why drama?"

"Because," I said, "drama is like comedy but without the jokes."

Mrs. Horowitz was far from amused. She gave me a severe look. "I suppose," she said, "that your jokes are nothing to write home about."

"Telling them is a dangerous proposition," I said, with a shrug. "If no one laughs at the punch line, that's the end of the story."

She said nothing. Instead she took a deep breath, perhaps to control a sense of contempt, so that—except for the vein pulsing at the side of her forehead, under the elaborately teased hair—it would not overtake her.

"So," I went on to say, "drama is safer."

"Listen here, Dostoyevsky," she said. "Let me tell you: the last thing my daughter needs is to be involved with a would-be writer."

I gasped as Natasha cried, "Mama!"

Which did nothing to slow Mrs. Horowitz down. "In every family," she said, "one genius is enough, no, on second thought, it's more than enough. Two are a recipe for disaster, because they'll end up starving to death and blaming each other for it."

I thought of saying that having died of starvation would not leave these geniuses enough juice for exchanging accusations, as there could be no pointing fingers from beyond the grave, but to be on the safe side I decided not to offer my opinion on the subject.

Mrs. Horowitz went on. "As long as I'm here, Natasha can rest assured that I'll sacrifice myself not only to advance her career and her fame but also to put food on the table and provide for shelter overhead. But I won't live forever—"

"Ma, please—"

"So now," said Mrs. Horowitz, "what are your intentions, may I ask, regarding my daughter?"

Surprised that she leveled this question at me, which she did before I even had a real opportunity to have a conversation with Natasha, I said, "Mrs. Horowitz, let me assure you about my intentions. They're utterly serious—"

"That's what I'm afraid of," she said, waving her hand at me. "I'm not going to allow Natasha to marry anyone coming off the street, even if he arrived in a luxury car, especially not someone who has some vague dreams of writing drama for no better reason than he's no good at jokes."

Before I could answer that no one had been discussing marriage yet, and it was much too early to bring up the subject now, "Mama," said the girl, in her most stubborn tone, "I can make up my own mind, thank you very much."

With that, Natasha sat down at her piano, raised her hands over the keys, and with great gusto, pounded them till the upside-down skyline of Manhatten trembled in the polished surface.

＊

Mrs. Horowitz marched off to the kitchen, leaving us alone at long last.

"Play for me, Natasha," I said.

She turned her eyes to me, and the green light in them flickered into a smile.

"What kind of music d'you like?" she asked.

To which I said, "I'd like to know what you like."

"My favorite is The Symphony No. 5 in C minor by Ludwig van Beethoven," she said, "but this is not the right moment for it. I know! I'll play a special song for you. Papa used to sing it to me, when I was little."

The first notes came softly, tugging at my heart. They brought back long-forgotten Yiddish words, in the voice of my mother. "Bei mir bist du shein[4]," she sang to me. "Bei mir host du chein. Bei mir bist du alles oif di velt."

Natasha closed her eyes, surrendering herself to the music. She started swaying slightly as she played and from time to time, tipped her head backwards, letting it wash over her face, her lips. Fascinated I found myself drawing nearer. By the rosy blush that spread up her cheeks I knew that she could sense my closeness.

In her soft, velvety voice, she started singing, "To me you are beautiful, to me you have grace, to me you are everything in the world."

From the direction of the kitchen, her Ma chimed in, singing, "I've tried to explain, bei mir bist du schoen."

And in a sudden elation I hummed under my breath, "So kiss me, and say that you will understand."

With the last notes still hovering in midair, she swung her knees around the piano bench and lifted her face to

---

[4] Bei Mir Bistu Shein composed by Jacob Jacobs (lyricist) and Sholom Secunda (composer) in 1932.

me. I raised her to her feet and gathered her to my heart. Then, as she wrapped her arms around my shoulders, I felt the heat awakening from within, rising recklessly in both of us.

Drawing me to her, Natasha leaned backwards over the piano. To the last vibrations dying in its belly I bent over her, over the reflection of the skyline of New York, which rippled in reverse across the polished, black surface around us, and I kissed her.

The Fifth

Chapter 10

When I left Natasha that evening and walked away from her doorstep, the last thing on my mind was what to say to Uncle Shmeel about the damage I had caused, by accident, to his convertible. That dread would come later—or rather, it was waiting for me to come to it, but for now, the only thing that pervaded me, pervaded my entire existence, was a sudden daze of happiness. Oh, and the other thing, too: my lips. To me they felt as if they were on fire. I would not be surprised if some passerby would point at them and tell me that they were swollen, distended to the point of taking over my entire face.

Despite sounding like a cliché, the feeling was overwhelmingly real. I was grateful that her Mama had not bothered to see me to the door, because then she would have realized, without a doubt, that I had just kissed her daughter.

As it turned out Uncle Shmeel noticed the dent in the front of the car at a single glance, before I had a chance to open my mouth and tell him about it.

"What happened?" he asked. "You all right?"

"I'm fine," said I. "And don't worry, I'm going to pay you back for the damage, I promise I will, every single penny—"

"Ah," he said, waving a hand at me. "Forget it! Now that it's scratched I can start driving this thing without fear of wrecking something that is too damn pristine."

"I'm going to pay you anyway, just as soon as I find myself back to camp and get my pay—"

"Which reminds me," he said. "D'you have a train ticket to go back?"

"No—"

"D'you have enough money for a train ticket?"

"No—"

"Just as I thought," said Uncle Shmeel, stuffing a roll of dollar bills into my pocket. "Well, now you do!"

Then, over my stunned loss for words, he went on to say, "So? Tell me everything!"

"About what?"

"How did it go with the girl?"

"Oh," I said vaguely. "We just talked—"

"Is that all you did?"

"For the most part."

"What did you talk about, then?"

"Oh nothing, just this, that, and the other thing."

"Such as?"

"Music."

"Ah! How romantic! Did you serenade her?"

"No, she played the piano for me."

"And you forgot to tell her, didn't you, that I used to make a living by playing the clarinet?"

"No, yes, I mean—"

Uncle Shmeel picked up his instrument and for emphasis, shook it in the air. "Perhaps," he said, "you'll tell her next time."

"Perhaps I will," said I. "If I'm lucky enough to have a next time."

"So?" he said. "What kind of music does she like?"

"Her favorite," I told him, "is Symphony No. 5 in C minor by Ludwig van Beethoven."

"Ah," he said, nodding his head with appreciation. "The Fifth! This girl has class!"

Then, tightening his lips over the mouthpiece of his woodwind instrument and blowing his cheeks, he sounded the opening phrase with great, quivering pathos.

Dit-dit-dit-dah...

I raised my hand for a farewell handshake, as I had to catch the last train out of town, but according to Uncle Shmeel, the conversation had only begun, so why rush it?

And without losing a beat he started telling me, between one momentous blow and another, that thirty years after it was written, this rhythm was used for the letter *V* in Morse code, and therefore it would surely come to represent the notion of victory, thanks in part to the BBC, because since the beginning of this war it had started to preface its broadcasts with those four notes, played on drums, but if you would ask him—

which for some reason, no one cared to do—he could give it more punch, not only because the clarinet had the largest ranges of pitch of all musical instruments but also because no other *Kleismer* could hope to come close to the way he played it, which might sound like bragging but really, it wasn't.

You can hear it for yourself, can't you? Dit-dit-dit-dah!

At this point Uncle Shmeel smoothed his hair over his bald spot and took a long, deep breath, which allowed him to go on explaining that at any rate, this new interpretation of the symphony would have surprised the composer himself, as did the other, more common interpretation, which was based on the rumor that he, Beethoven, had pointed to the beginning of the first movement and said, "Thus fate knocks at the door."

Fascinating as that might have sounded it was completely wrong, nothing more than a fancy myth, but no one but Beethoven could have refuted it, which he had neglected to do, perhaps on account of being deaf, or mad, or both. And the truth was entirely different, you see, and much plainer. It was not the idea of fate that had inspired him, nor was it Morse code, rather it was the song of a yellow-hammer bird, which he had heard—penetrating, somehow, the heavy silence in his ears—while walking in Prater park in Vienna, which had been free to the public thanks to a declaration, a regal decree dating back to 1766 by Emperor Joseph II. And to make a short story long, the conclusion—dit-dit-dit-dah!—the conclusion is this: when two ideas compete for popular attention, fate would always get the upper hand, especially when its rival is merely a songbird.

Uncle Shmeel took another breath, but before he could convert it into words I caught his hand and shook it, thanking him for his wonderful help and for not killing me over what I had done to his 1941 Ford Super Deluxe Convertible.

With that I took leave of him and made it to the station just in time for the last train.

Upon arrival at Camp Lejeune I had not a moment to catch my breath. I was called to the office at once.

"Listen up," said the officer. "So far this war, the Battle of the Atlantic is our longest continuous military campaign, having started in 1939. We're constantly sending re-enforcements, but as for you—"

"Yes sir?"

"You're going to join the operation of the London Detachment."

I knew these orders were coming, but when they did I was not ready for them. Even so I snapped to attention.

"At ease," he ordered.

Making an effort to relax, which had no chance but failing, I said, "Yes sir."

And he said, "D'you know what's the most essential qualification for Marine selected for this operation?"

"No sir. What is it?"

"It's the desire to be one."

At this point I couldn't help but cut in. "Sir," I said. "Please, refresh my memory: when have you asked me about my desire —"

"I haven't," said the officer. "And I'm not about to ask you now. Now don't interrupt me when I'm talking—"

"No sir, I won't."

He raised a hairy eyebrow.

"Those selected," he said, "should be fairly young but stable. They should be conscientious, cool-headed but aggressive--"

"Doesn't that immediately rule me out?"

"Even if it does, I want you out of my hair. So go ahead, gather your things."

"Sir?"

"Start packing."

"When?"

"Right now! This afternoon."

"Where—"

"The London Detachment resides in a non-military facility on Grosvenor Square, close to the American Embassy. This place," he said, "is not without risk. Serving as a symbol of our country, it's a tempting target for the German enemy."

"One more question—"

"What?"

"What's the mission?"

"It's modeled after a similar mission in Shanghai, China, back in 1937. You are to provide security for the American embassy and to provide escort for State Department couriers, operating between the Embassy and various governmental staff offices in London."

"And sir, one more thing—"

"What?"

"What equipment do I need?"

"You're going to get a Harley-Davidson motorcycle equipped with sidecars to operate the courier service."

"Really?" I asked, with a sudden spark of delight.

And he said, "Really."

Which made me imagine myself already there. In my mind I rehearsed every motion, every single part of every motion, mounting one of these bad boys. Leaning against the bike I would put my entire weight onto the left leg, lift the right one over it, then adjust the mirror. And twisting the right hand grip towards my body I would apply throttle, starting the engine.

Having gained momentum I would put both feet up onto the foot pegs. Accelerating, shifting, breaking, turning! The wind would scream, it would brush, ever so crisply, though the bristles of my hair as I would cruise down the streets, round the squares, cross the bridge over the river Thames. One moment I would be riding at the head of a motorcycle formation, the next—riding solo, on my way to Big Ben. Oh, what a thrill!

"Sir," I said. "I wonder—"

"No more questions," said the officer. "Go, get ready. You're scheduled to leave in less than four hours."

Preparing myself for a new adventure started out as an incredible thrill, but ended on a note of uncertainty. After all, London was lighting up, literally: the Blitz, a period of sustained strategic bombing of the United Kingdom by Nazi Germany, was quite a spectacular thing, thanks to the earlier work of German legal scholars of the 1930's. They had carefully worked out guidelines for what type of bombing was permissible under international law, ruling out direct attacks against civilians, but accepting the concept of attacking vital war industries, at the cost of heavy civilian casualties and breakdown of civilian morale.

This—right here, right now—was a trying moment for me. Because of the war, because of the way it would destroy some lives and forever change others, I felt, all of a sudden, a pang of fear. Who could tell the future? I might never have another chance to talk with my sweetheart. Perhaps our first kiss was destined to be the last.

"No," I told myself, "don't even think it. Nonsense. There's no reason to worry. Even from a distance, a measure of closeness can be maintained. We'll go on writing to each other. I'll come back. She'll wait for me."

Having packed my stuff I leapt at the last chance to call Natasha. This time, the phone was picked up at the first ring, by her Mama.

"You again," she grumbled.

And at once, "Who is it?" called the girl, somewhere in the background.

"Unfortunately," said Mrs. Horowitz to her daughter, "it's him."

And as if to form a sound barrier between us, she bellowed in my ear, with the full blast of her Russian accent, "So? What shall I tell her? What's the reason you're calling?"

"Would you let me talk to her?"

"Why should I?"

"Because" I told her, "I got my orders. I mean, I have to leave, heading for London, so—"

"London?" she said, and then demanded, in a cut-and-dry tone, "when?"

"Soon," I said, glancing at my watch. "My departure time is in less than three hours."

"Young man, war is not as glorious as you might expect, and neither is that city."

"I know—"

"That place," she said, "is all wrong. Like driving on the left side of the road, and having money based on an archaic, impossible accounting system, and drinking warm beer."

"I know—"

"Do you? Some buildings are in complete ruins, others have tomatoes growing on the rooftops, because people are worried that supplies may soon become scarce."

"Mrs. Horowitz, I've seen photographs in the newspaper, just this morning."

"Have you? Many of the streets are bomb-scarred. It's a sad, dangerous place."

"I must go. It's my duty," I said, feeling awkward. "And I have no idea, right now, when I can call again, so—"

"There you go," said Mrs. Horowitz, directing her voice away from the phone, back to her daughter. "Just as I thought! Men! Here today, gone tomorrow."

"Mama," said the girl, in an agonized voice. "It's his duty."

The woman started clicking her tongue.

"Indeed," she said, between one click and another. "And when it's all over, what d'you think is going to happen? Don't you know?"

The girl gave no answer, so her Mama pressed on. "Distance changes things. Old flames cool off, new ones flare up. Perhaps he'll come back, months, even years from now, with a young English bride hanging pretty on his arm. Have you given it any thought?"

"No," said Natasha, in a stubborn tone. "I haven't. And I'm not going to do any thinking, not now, not any time soon."

"Mrs. Horowitz," I cut in, pleading. "Let me talk to your daughter, let me say goodbye to her—"

I heard a gasp as Natasha reached for the phone and took hold of it.

"Here I am," she said.

For a moment we just stood there, listening for each other's breath. Then she said, "I don't even know why it hurts so much."

And I said, "I'll write to you, sweetheart."

"Yes," said Natasha. "I'll be waiting."

"No," said her Mama, putting her foot down. "Not if I can help it!"

We heard the sound of her slippers slapping against the floor. When at last it faded, I said, "Play for me, Natasha."

I expected her to ask, "What shall I play," but she didn't.

First I heard a soft touch. She must have set the receiver not in its usual place away from the piano, but right on top of it, so that not only my ear but also my entire being would sense every vibration. Then, in a burst, came a sequence of notes, which sounded familiar, even though their sound resonated in a manner that was entirely different, and much more powerful from that of the clarinet. It was The Fifth.

Dit-dit-dit-dah...

The music came, it rose into my ear and descended into my heart. It made me forget where I was, where I had to be going. At first I recalled that it had been inspired by the song of a yellow-hammer, or perhaps by the way fate would knock at the door. Then I left these interpretations far behind. My mind filled with radiant beams that shot through the gloom, bringing gigantic shadows that rocked back and forth, forth and back. They were closing in on me, aiming to destroy everything from within, everything except the pain of longing, endless longing to which I had to succumb.

In a climax that climbed on and on Natasha led me forward into another universe, and then far beyond, into the infinite. To me she was no longer a girl. A muse, that was what she became.

I was stirred—deeply, intimately—by the solemn yearning for something I could not even put in words. And until the final chord—and the moments that followed it—I remained paralyzed, powerless to step out of her spell, out of this silence she imposed upon me, where grief and joy come, rushing in from opposite ends, to meet.

After a long while, "Goodbye, Lenny," she said, softly.

"Wait," I said. "What is it you're thinking about, when you play like that?"

"If I tell you, you'll think me crazy."

"If you don't, my own sanity will be gone."

"I've never revealed this to anyone, not even to my Pa," she said. "Only when at last he forgot who I was, when he deteriorated into being stony, did I whisper my thoughts to him. Why did I do it? Perhaps I wanted to shock him into coming back, into talking to me, recognizing who I was. Or else, perhaps I wanted to ease his fears—the way I imagined them—because it was time for him to go."

"He taught you how to play this piece, didn't he?"

"Pa used to say that playing the notes correctly was only a small part of performing. Memorization was important, but even more so was learning how to immerse myself, how to become the spirit of the music, especially when it's dark."

"You make me so curious," I said, and hesitated to add, "so in the end, when he forgot who you were, what did you whisper to him?"

"You don't want to hear this."

"I do."

She took a deep breath.

Then, in a low voice, she said, "I told him that when I play this music I think of myself as Death."

Amazed at the way her mind worked I said nothing. Beethoven's Fifth, evoking the image of Fate knocking at the door, was a dark piece, and darkly did she play it. Which told me one thing: there was something about her, something I could not define, except to say that it startled me.

If I had my wits about me—which I didn't, because of the passion, the memory of her touch, her kiss—if I were free to think with any degree of clarity I should forget her and find me a simpler girl.

In my silence Natasha went on to say, "I told him, close your eyes, Pa."

"Here I am," I said, "closing mine."

"Now, Lenny, imagine hearing the music. At the sound of it, can you see me coming, wearing a shroud, which flutters long behind me in the wind and captures the last rays of sunset? Can you see me floating towards you, all through the night? I'm so powerful, then. And forlorn. And aching to make you happy, by taking you out where I am, into the darkness, faraway from all trouble, all misery."

I was too overwhelmed to speak.

"Perhaps this is not what you expected to hear," said Natasha. "But it's the way I feel. It is the truth."

"And I love you for it."

Her last words to me were barely audible.

I think they were, "I'll be thinking about you, Lenny."

Always Remember

Chapter 11

I t was not immediately that I noticed the silence between Natasha and me. Finding myself on the other side of the Atlantic Ocean I ached to read her words, to detect her whisper rising to me from the paper. I figured that her letters would take time. They would have to be redirected from Camp Lejeune to our compound here. And so I told myself to be patient.

That night, as I landed in a darkened airport outside London, I imagined my father back home, bent closely over the radio, wishing to protect me by learning every hint, every rumor, every report about the European front. He would shush the neighbors and ignore their complaints about his raising the volume when it was time for the news. Perhaps he thought I could just hear it, at full blast, all the way across the ocean.

In his last letter to me he had explained that as an island nation, the United Kingdom was highly dependent on imported goods: a million tons per week, simply in order to be able to survive. Meanwhile, the Germans attempted to stem the flow of merchant shipping that enables Britain to go on, to keep fighting.

This time, his letter sounded verbose, to the point of being overwhelming. But underneath this unusual excess of facts, facts, and more facts, I had caught his tone. There could be no other name for it but prayer.

Arriving at dusk I saw the city enter its blackout. It was a different place than I had imagined, a gloomy one. Gone were the famously bright lights of Piccadilly Circus, a public space of the city's west end. It looked utterly deserted. The houses looked grimy. They had not been painted since the beginning of the war in 1939, because factories were not making paint—they were making planes.

The next morning, walking through the war-ravaged city, I noticed children having a good time playing in the rubble, which had been scattered in the street in the wake of last night's air raid.

I wrote to my father, saying that the people here were amazingly resilient and planned ahead for survival. Huge emergency water tanks were being filled, in hopes of sustaining this metropolitan during a siege. In public parks and gardens, acres of allotments had been reassigned to growing foods. To my surprise I spotted vegetables growing there, between the beds of roses.

Beautiful, decorative railings around buildings and along the Thames river were being removed—you might even say, sacrificed—for the purpose of fashioning them into weapons.

To me it looked like the end of the world, only in reverse: plowshares beaten into swords, and pruning hooks into spears.

At noon Trafalgar Square was bustling with Allied servicemen, wearing the uniforms of twenty different nations. Most of them were marching around, looking for action. I stood there, under Nelson's column, pretending to be playing a role, an unscripted role in some heroic movie, protecting the British Commonwealth and by doing so, protecting the entire free world.

Meanwhile, one English girl after another would come by and offer a smile or a flower, which made me feel wanted.

"We love you," said one girl.

"You're my hero," said another.

My heart swelled. Of course, the Harley-Davidson motorcycle, which had been given to me upon arrival at the London Detachment, added to the thrill.

Within days I became highly proficient at riding it, hoping that my officers would not pay attention to my stunts. A spectacle, that's what I was: roaring through alleys, dodging rubble, and for an extra kick, standing on the saddle while lifting the front of the motorcycle off the ground.

All that action served me well. It distracted my mind from a growing unease, somewhere deep inside. I was fearless not only because of my love of adventure and not only because I enjoyed riding the beast but also because of a sense of emptiness. The hope to hear from Natasha had started to harden into despair.

Also, no letters arrived from my father, despite the fact that he had usually written to me every week.

In fact, I was becoming too fearless for my own good, because my daring manner of maneuvering the bike brought about new orders for departure, away from both the bike and the city of London. I was chosen, along with ten other enlisted men and two of the officers, for training that was modeled after the highly acclaimed British commando methods. We arrived at Achnacarry, Scotland, where our exercise schedule proceeded regardless of weather, which was nothing to write home about. It was poor.

We were quartered in prefabricated huts that were made of corrugated iron, shaped into half cylinders. We slept on wooden slabs laid across six-inch blocks, with straw mats in place of mattresses. During seven grueling weeks, our practice went on around the clock: Bren guns, grenades, pistols, Thompson submachine guns, foreign arms, Garand rifles, and all over again. Bren guns, grenades, pistols...

In addition there were even more intensive sessions: physical training, scouting, patrolling, map reading, toggle bridging, and all over again. Physical training, scouting, patrolling...

We crossed a stream by using a fifty-foot rope ladder to climb a tree, and from there sliding down a taut rope stretched downwards at a thirty degree angle, to reach the opposite bank. For descending from cliffs, we used a hundred foot length of rope, looped around a rock. We climbed down in bounds, and brought the rope section along with each increment of descent. Then we crawled under a barbed wire, ascended a log ramp in order to jump from an eight-foot height over some barbed wire obstacle, and finished the course with a bayonet charge.

A rapid, seven-mile march topped it all off. It demanded extreme endurance, as all men had to keep in step, which was meant to create teamwork. By the end of it I felt like a part in a well-oiled machine, moving at to its beat, surrendering to its purpose, whatever that might be. I no longer felt as an individual.

My mind seemed to have gone numb. The only thing that would bring me back into myself was my longing for Natasha.

Despite my exhaustion I wrote her a letter almost every evening. It included nothing, not a word about what I was going through, because I assumed that these mundane details about our training methods would be boring, utterly boring to her, and on the flip side, they would be of particular interest to the German enemy, should the letter fall, somehow, into their hands.

So I limited myself to sweet nothings, hoping that Natasha would find pleasure, somehow, in my writing, and that it would not fall into the hands of my bigger, more formidable enemy: her Mama.

I wrote,

> *Last night I was invited into a Scottish home and the host urged me to eat up, saying, "Look, there's plenty on the table!" "You sure?" I asked, and with a smile he answered, "Sure I'm sure!"*
>
> *Even so I should have gone easy. The next morning I figured that what I ate was probably the family's rations for an entire week, which they spread out to show hospitality.*

A week passed, then a month, then forever went by. There was no answer. Not a single letter arrived from Natasha. Again I tried to explain away her silence. I told myself that once a letter would come out of the NJ post office and make its way to Camp Lejeune, it would have to be redirected from there to the London Detachment and then to Achnacarry, Scotland, which might cause it to be lost anywhere along the line.

I decided not to worry.

Having completed our commando training we returned to London to await our next orders. I went back to my Marine Security Guard duty, which was considered a prestigious assignment, available to qualified Marines. It allowed me to ride my motorcycle all over the city. During one of the air raids it had been blasted from under me by flying debris. I got up from the dirt, dusted myself off, and delivered messages afoot, limping.

I tried to call Natasha a few times, but when I managed, after several frustrating tries, to get the telephone operator, she said there was something wrong with the number.

"No," I insisted. "That's the right number, I'm sure of it."

"Perhaps," she suggested, "it had been disconnected?"

"That can't be," I insisted. "Did you try again?"

"Yes," she said. "I did."

I could not even begin to guess what had happened, nor could I figure out a way to contact Natasha.

Meanwhile I got a new bike. Around the same time I became friends with Ryan, an enlisted man who had arrived from Detroit, only a month ago. We were idling about next to our non-military facility, which was located on Grosvenor Square, close to the American Embassy. It was then that—to my surprise—I noticed him stuffing a letter, which carried American stamps, into his shirt pocket. It irked me to learn that unlike me, he was getting mail, on a regular basis, from back home.

I wondered out loud, "How come I'm not getting any letters?"

"Well," he said. "Someone has to be writing them."

"I do have someone," said I. "A girlfriend."

"You do?" he asked. "How long have you been dating her?"

Which confused me, because by his measure of things, Natasha and I had not been going steady at all, and our relationship was little more than imaginary, as it amounted to a single kiss.

In response to my silence, "I see," he said.

"See what?"

"She's not as serious about you as you've hoped she would be, is she now?"

I said nothing.

So he pressed on. "Whatever happened between the two of you, perhaps it's been just a fling."

"Perhaps," I said, "you shouldn't stick your nose in my affairs."

"Oh, stop being a dreamer! Wake up! Look around you!"

"What is there to see?"

"So many cute babes here, and they all adore us and want to have a little chat, which is a bit hard to understand, because they speak with that fascinating, mind-bending foreign accent, which makes me forget the name of my girlfriend back home."

"It does? Really?"

"Really. I have to ask myself, What's her name? And then I recall, Oh yes, it's Lana. I used to be shy around girls, but no more!"

I shrugged, saying nothing.

So he pointed out at the gals at the other side of the square. "You see? They're here for the taking. And as for your girlfriend, well, she's back there."

"Oh," I said. "I know the way you think, know it all too well—"

"And so does Lana," said Ryan, snorting a laugh. "That's why she's worried. That's why she keeps writing."

Again I said nothing, and he went on.

"The important thing," he added, by way of giving advice, "is not to make any promises. I never talk about my plans, and when she does, all I say about the future revolves around my military career. I tell her that after three years as a Marine Security Guard I'll be entitled to the Marine Corps Security Guard Ribbon or a service star."

Listlessly I said, "Who cares? I never talk about ribbons and stars with Natasha."

"Oh Lenny," he said, shaking his head. "I can see how much you miss her."

I said nothing a third time, because what was the point in saying, "I do."

So he suggested, "How about making your babe jealous? Have you thought about that?"

"Natasha is different from other girls. She's a pianist, a rising star."

"Oh, now that explains it!"

"Explains what?"

"Don't you see? She's in show business."

"So?"

"So?" he repeated, as if there was no need to explain anything beyond that single word. "So she meets men, handsome men, all the time! They're always around her: actors, musicians, singers, dancers, conductors, producers, stage managers, music hall directors, composers, and others, all of whom have more in common with her than you'll ever do!"

At hearing this, a sudden weakness came over me, which Ryan must have noticed, because his tone changed.

"There, there," he said, and gave me a pat on the shoulder. "Do yourself a favor, don't pray for a letter from her, much less faithfulness."

I took a step back from him, mounted my bike, and bolted away from there, producing hellish noise for no better reason than to drown his advice, but to my dismay it went on rattling, rattling, rattling inside me.

I rode for a long while and when at last I came back to my quarters, surprise! There was an envelope on my pillow, and it was from my father.

My first thought was that by arriving here, this letter served to prove a point. It showed me that I was reachable. If you wanted to contact me, you could, which meant for some reason, Natasha didn't. She must have stopped caring for me. What else could explain the silence of my muse?

My second thought was not exactly a thought. Rather, it was a jolt of alarm. I could see, quite plainly, that his handwriting had changed. It was with a shaky, trembling hand that my dad wrote,

Lenny my son, I wish I could go on keeping this from you, but at this point I can no longer do it. I'm in pain, severe pain, and it's been wrecking me for the past three months.

You know me, I've always resisted—perhaps too stubbornly—to set an appointment with my doctor, because despite being a learned man, he can never help, and all he does, in my opinion, is rely on the wisdom of ignorants and prescribe drugs for them, drugs for which the unintended side effects are worse than the disease they're supposed to cure.

At last the pain became unbearable, so I dragged myself, somehow, to his office, and after a long series of exams I finally got a diagnosis, and Lenny, it's not good.

Too bad you're so far away. I know that the Battle of the Atlantic is a crucial one. I heard Winston Churchill call it, 'the longest, largest, and most complex naval battle in history.'

I know you're doing your duty there, and for that I'm proud of you, son. Thinking of you I read the paper every day, but find myself too tired to cut clippings out of it and send them to you, which may seem to be a simple task, but for me, it's daunting. Besides, there's no real need for these clippings, is there, because you are right there, in the thick of things.

From listening to the radio I've learned a lot about the war. The Germans seek to prevent the buildup of Allied supplies and equipment in the British Isles in preparation for the invasion of occupied Europe.

This cause, fighting an evil enemy who threatens to overtake the entire world, is greater than both of us. So the last thing I would want is to take you away from where you are, by asking you to come back home to see me.

The words *one last time* did not appear on the paper, but I knew they must have been weighing on his heart. Perhaps that was why the letter was left unfinished.

In place of a signature he scribbled,

I miss you. Always remember—

Amazing Grace

Chapter 12

I was shocked to realize how gravely sick my dad was, and how long he had kept it from me. Hoping it was not too late for me to see him I went to the two officers in charge and requested permission for an urgent leave, which to my surprise I got, as soon as I presented his letter. Perhaps they were touched by what he had written, but on top of that they had another reason, beyond giving me a chance to see my father. They must have decided that my return to the States would serve a greater purpose.

"Permission granted," said one officer. "You can go back home. You can even stay in New York for a couple of months and take care of your father."

"But," said the second officer, "before that, you'll have to do one thing for us."

"Yes sir," I said. "What would it be?"

He didn't answer at once. Instead he said, "I'm sure you know that the Allied forces have managed to damage many of the German U-boats, to break the blockade. We've done it at great cost. Many of our own merchant ships and warships have sunk, thanks to the navy of Nazi Germany, the Kriegsmarin, and thanks to the air force of their allies, the Japanese. Our casualties are mounting."

Meanwhile the other officer turned to the back wall, where a naval map of the world displayed oceans, vast oceans layered with blues of varying intensity, in which I noticed a scattering of red pins.

"The USS Tucker, a destroyer," he said, pointing at one pin, "struck a mine back in August, here, in the Pacific Ocean. The Kaimoku, a US cargo ship, was torpedoed here, in the Atlantic Ocean. And over there," he said, pointing at another pin, "in the Battle of Guadalcanal, the USS Astoria was shelled by Japanese cruisers."

"More recently, the George Tucker, a cargo ship on her maiden voyage, was torpedoed and damaged in the Atlantic Ocean, off the shores of Africa. Survivors were rescued by two Free French Naval forces. She burnt for days and sank on November the third."

"Each one of these pins," said the first officer, "represents more than a time and place. It represents men lost at sea. Few bodies were recovered."

"I know it, sir," said I. "Several of those who've trained with me have been brought back. They're buried here, in England, with a simple mark on their grave."

"Which brings us back to your mission," he said.

"What is it, sir?"

"To escort a coffin."

I hesitated to say, "Not sure I understand."

But then, in a blink, I recalled a rumor... An odd, persistent rumor, suggesting that the Navy decided to dig up the remains of soldiers and send them back home, because of some film, a documentary that was shocking even to servicemen, let alone civilians, why? Because it included close-up views of the faces of dead soldiers as they had been being loaded into body bags. By some accounts it was unflinching in its realism, which had been unheard of up to now, in both fictional portrayals of war as well as newsreel footage.

The two officers noted my silence. They glanced at each other, then at me.

"You'll accompany the coffin," said on of them, "until it's turned over to the mortuary of the family's choosing."

And the other one said, "We must show the grieving families, and the nation at large, that the fallen are treated with dignity."

"Yes sir," I said. "I'll do it."

Yet my willingness to fulfill what was requested of me came with heavy doubts. In accepting it I felt as if I were flanked by trouble: anxiety for my dying father on one side, and for the fallen soldier on the other. Everywhere I went, everywhere I turned, there was the presence of death.

I kept telling myself that it didn't matter. Whatever happened in my life was unimportant, it was negligible compared to all the casualties of this horrific war, all the damage inflicted not only here in London but also throughout Europe and throughout the entire world. The map was filling in with more and more red pins.

I was angry with myself for feeling lost. And what made it so much worse was the grim sense of living, somehow, in a void, which was all that remained once I realized that my affair, for lack of a better word, with Natasha was over. Perhaps it was never meant to be. Unable to stop thinking about her I convinced myself that she had made no effort to reach me. Given no reason to believe otherwise I grew bitter. I blamed her for the way I found myself now, alone and drifting.

I was not even planning on visiting her upon my return to the States. If she would come out I would not be there, would not make a fool of myself by waiting outside her fence. I'm damned, I said to myself, if I would try to break her door down. Instead I decided to move on, arming myself with the memory of that time, that one evening when she played so beautifully, to tell me that to her I was everything in the world. Of course, I could only believe that it was a figure of speech, demanded by the lyrics of the song.

By now I had stopped sending letters and tried, as hard as I could, to forget her. I did my best to put her music out of my mind, to silence it.

But the more I tried the more I heard that echo, the echo of her voice coming at me, rebounding over and again, promising, "I'll be waiting."

In truth, why should I feel disappointed? Many of the soldiers around me were in the habit of betraying the trust of their dear ones and suspected they were, in turn, being betrayed. That was the way things were, and to believe otherwise was simply naive.

Perhaps in time, the pain would subside. My passion for Natasha would slowly be turning to ashes. It would lose the last tinge of color, of hope. There were the remains of a body in the flag-draped coffin that was about to be entrusted to me, and the remains of love in my heart.

On my flight back to New York, a new worry occurred to me. I dreaded having to face the grieving parents. How would I find the words to comfort them? What should I say if they ask if I had known Charlie, their son? What could I tell them about his last moments?

To prepare myself I ran over his story, over and again, in my mind. The details were rough, they were quite sketchy, because I had learnt them only a day ago, from a survivor of that battle.

He had told me, "That night, the seas were running a little high. It was kind of a bad situation right off the start. We headed to the rubber boats for a dash to the beach. For a while, we bounced around in the surf, then drifted ashore, because only three of the outboard motors would start. We braced ourselves for what was to come, as well-rehearsed plans gave way to improvisation."

"Then, one of us accidentally fired his weapon, eliminating any hope of surprising the enemy. We lined up across the narrow strip of land and started walking. Soon we saw the Germans coming. We fired at them. They fired at us over a distance of 20 yards. Charlie was the first one to be hit."

What could I tell his parents if they ask why, why did it have to happen to him?

Coming off the plane I noticed a group of three silent figures and by their deathly pale faces I recognized them: his mother, father, and pregnant wife. They stood together, strangely separated from the hustle bustle of the airport, waiting for me.

They watched in solemn silence as I wheeled the casket toward them. It was a tense moment. No questions were asked, no tears shed. The mother, still reeling from the shock of losing her son, did not cry. Instead she bit her lips, hard. The father wrapped his arm around her for support, but he was the one that seemed closest to the verge of collapse.

Then he steadied himself, somehow, and with a gentle motion, stroked the flag that wrapped the coffin.

"So sorry for your loss," I said, feeling awkward for using a phrase that was too weak and all too common to convey what I was feeling.

He nodded his head to signal that he heard me, but neither he nor the mother could utter a single word. In their place, the soldier's young wife came to me, holding something in her hand.

Softly she said, "When Charlie came home on his last leave, he gave me the Marine Corps emblem off his hat. At first I refused it, knowing that without the emblem, he risked not being readmitted to the base."

I said, "Perhaps he had a premonition of what would come his way and wanted you to keep it."

"Yes," she whispered, clutching it to her heart. "I still have it. It's a cherished memento."

Meanwhile, from out of nowhere, a lone bagpiper came by. In the midst of a busy airport he looked like an apparition from a different place and time, marching slowly towards us. As he strolled past the flag-draped casket I caught the music he was playing: it was an old song, written by an Englishman who in the early part of his life had been an outspoken atheist, libertine, and slave trader, only to find his faith after riding out a storm at sea.

Amazing Grace.[5]

The sound of it was magical. It quelled the noise of people fussing, people walking all about, rushing to and fro with suitcases and stuff. At the same time it calmed the silence, the angry silence in my heart, opening it anew to sadness and to joy.

It was then that the soldier's wife took a step forward to the casket and placed the emblem on it, which for her meant the beginning of farewell, and for the fallen, the end of a long journey, the journey home.

Her voice trembled as she started singing for him,

> Amazing grace... How sweet the sound
> That saved a wretch like me
> I once was lost, but now am found
> Was blind, but now I see.

Her voice was so soft, so heartbreakingly delicate, and yet it made the hair rise on my head and the flesh quiver on my bones. I felt—oh, I can't explain what I felt! It was not only grief for this man, who was a brother of mine even though I had never come to know him, but also pity for his family and for all us, civilians and soldiers, the fallen, the wounded, the loved ones back home, all the lives forever changed by this horrific war.

In my childhood, my mother used to sing *Amazing Grace* to me in place of a lullaby, because it had always calmed me down before she tucked me in, before she said good night.

---

[5] Amazing Grace written by John Newton in 1748

Through many dangers, toils and snares,

I have already come

'Tis grace hath brought me safe thus far,

And grace will lead me home.

The music made me think of Natasha. In a complete reversal of emotion I found myself overcoming my rage, my sense of betrayal. Suddenly I realized that whatever had caused the break between us should be set aside. It was time to accept and be accepted in return.

I, too, was coming home.

And I could not wait to see my father.

To Find Myself Forsaken

Chapter 13

The smell of dank earth filled my nostrils as I stood over the open grave. Ashes to ashes, dust to dust, there was Charlie, coming home. There were his parents, awash with tears. And now that my task to accompany him to his final resting place had been completed, my thoughts turned back to my father. It was time for me to come home, too. I prayed it was not too late. Was there still time to say, I love you, dad?

I could have learned more about his present condition had I called Uncle Shmeel, but the thought of doing so did not occur to me, even as I spotted a phone booth in the distance, opposite the cemetery. I went out of there and sped away on the clunky motorcycle I had rented upon my arrival. The night was calm, and there was barely any traffic on my way to my father's apartment in South Bronx.

All the while I promised myself, with great fervor, that I would do everything my father had hoped for. I would register for the university, just as soon as my military service was over. I would get a degree, start a professional career, marry, and raise a family. If only I could see him one last time.

But unfortunately, this was not to happen.

When the door opened, there was Uncle Shmeel. I was shaken up to see him without his shoes, as was the custom in the old country to mourn for the dead. He didn't have to say a word. Somehow I leapt to the realization of what must have occurred, which made me feel as if the earth fell from under my feet.

Uncle Shmeel opened his arms and hugged me to his heart. Then he told me that my father had passed away and had been buried in a small ceremony, attended by close friends, nearly a week ago, which happened, I figured, before my flight had even landed on US soil.

"Then," I said, in a choked voice, "I came here for nothing."

"What d'you mean, for nothing? Am I chopped liver?" he asked. "Aren't you happy to see me?"

"I meant—"

"No worry, I understand. It's your father you wanted to see, not me. And not under these circumstances," said Uncle Shmeel. "He knew you'd come."

"Did he?"

"He asked me to apologize to you for him, because he simply couldn't take it any longer. He was in too much pain. It was time for him to give up."

I found myself lost somewhere between grief, confusion, and above all, anger: anger at him for not waiting long enough and anger at myself for failing to arrive here sooner.

I said nothing.

"He left this for you," said Uncle Shmeel, handing me a sealed envelope.

I took it. Still I said nothing.

"Well?" He nudged me. "Aren't you going to open it?"

131

"I don't know," I muttered. "No, not now."

That night, after Uncle Shmeel left, I went into my father's bedroom, opened his closet, and took out a metal hanger that held one of his shirts. White and airy, it reminded me of his presence. Stiffened with starch, the collar held its shape as if to fit around his neck. It smelled like him.

Gone was the anger. There was no one against whom I could rebel, which made me miss him even more.

I was glad that at long last, he had escaped the pain. I trusted, at that moment, that he was watching over me. The fabric swooshed this way and that, which made me feel him here, with me, around me.

Holding his shirt in front of me I glanced at the mirrored closet doors and saw much of him in myself. I hoped, I so hoped not to disappoint him in the future. He taught me well and expected great things of me.

I whispered, "I'm trying, dad. I really am."

The next day I went through all his papers, paid outstanding bills, and set aside my letters to him, which were neatly filed in his desk. I donated it and most of the furniture.

With great care I dusted off each one of his books, read the pages that he had earmarked, and played his records—all except one that seemed to be new. I left it in its original, sealed cover, because if he would never listen to it, why should I?

I stacked up the entire collection in the lobby of the building, and set up a hand-written sign that said, *FREE*. With that I gave it all away.

I felt compelled to busy myself with action and tried not to be swept away into memories, when I found some of my baby toys, which my father had kept in an old trunk all these years. I knocked at the next door and offered them to the neighbor.

"You sure?" said his kid.

"Sure I'm sure," said I.

With that I gave them all away.

By noontime the apartment was nearly empty. I was exhausted. It was beginning to feel like farewell not only to him but to my childhood as well.

In late afternoon I caught up on laundry, his and mine. When the clothes were dry, separated his shirts from mine and ironed them. Then I gave them away, all except one.

I hung it in the closet, and as if afraid I would lose him more than I already have, as if more of him were about to disappear, I placed it in front of mine. It hovered over me like a ghost, glowing in white even as evening shadows came slanting, longer and longer, across the room.

Sadness spread over me like a black stain. I sank to the floor but found myself unable to cry. It was there that at last I opened the envelope. To my surprise, two tickets fell out of it as I drew out his letter. In it he said,

I'm so glad you're here, Lenny.

Earlier this month I took a bus to the city and bought a pair of tickets for a show, a highly celebrated show in Carnegie Hall, no less. They were quite expensive but I didn't care. For once in my life I decided to splurge, even though—or maybe because—I knew that I wouldn't be able to join you.

When you arrive I may be gone. But I'm hoping that you will celebrate my life and our passion for music, which held us together through many of the letters we wrote to each other over the last few months, by not letting these tickets go to waste.

My seat may be empty, but I will be there by your side, listening.

It was a cold December evening, with gusty winds that made it feel even colder. The agitation of it fit my mood. In spite of my father's last request I was unsure if I should go to the concert. Bouts of grief came upon me even as I was escaping them by being busy. I worked frantically, around the clock, to sort out his things, sell most of them, and clean the vacant apartment in preparation to terminate his lease.

I felt tired, dejected. Going to a show was the last thing I would choose to do. Sitting next to an empty seat, surrounded by an audience that was cheerful and carefree, would distract me not only from my plans but also from my persistent thoughts, wondering if Natasha was thinking, from time to time, about me, and if so, was she whispering my name.

Going out would do me no good, or so I thought.

To my dismay, one of the neighbors had his radio playing at full blast, and a song came in, uninvited. I could not help but hearing the words, even though the window was closed.

> If you are made of air
> Upon your wing I'm taken
> Away from fear, despair
> To find myself forsaken

At hearing this I had to bolt out of the place, go elsewhere, anywhere. And so it was that at the last minute I decided, on a whim, to put on my father's white shirt and his only suit, which happened to fit me perfectly, and go check things out, tickets at hand.

Arriving at the corner of 7th Avenue and 57th Street I saw the massive building. Its exterior was rendered in narrow Roman bricks of a mellow ochre hue, with details accentuated in terra cotta and brownstone. Designed in the spirit of the Renaissance, Carnegie Hall was known as the most prestigious concert stage in the country, a place where leading classical music talents aspired to perform.

There, opposite me, stood men and women elegantly dressed, and by the clouds of breath that came out of their mouths, billowing in the chilly air, I knew they were chatting with each other. The crowd started flowing in to watch the performance. In somewhat of a daze I crossed the intersection and fell in line with all these fur coats.

Entering the place with them I found myself unprepared for the stunning elegance of the interior. It had a golden hue, an ambience of warmth and beauty.

A vaulted ceiling soared overhead. Not only was it breathtaking but also gave the hall its legendary acoustic sound. I recalled reading somewhere that the architect, who was an amateur cellist and treasurer of the Oratorio Society, had travelled to Europe to find out what makes a concert hall sound great.

For me, this was an awakening. My existence had sunk lately into a dead silence, that my senses had been deprived of light, music, or any touch of inspiration, but now, suddenly, something inside me stirred to life.

Bouncing about in my seat, which was the best one in the house—front row, center—I felt like a boy whose hunger had caught up to him and could not be denied anymore. Now I could not wait for the show to start.

"This place is amazing," said a soft, sultry voice in a slight Russian accent. "It's abuzz with excitement!"

I looked up. A young woman swung around in my direction, wearing full-length satin gloves that extended up above the elbows, a sparkly black evening dress with a slit on the side, and a necklace that dipped into her cleavage. Her hair swayed around her, shiny and bleached blond, as she gave a little nod to me. With a little sigh, she lowered herself into the empty seat.

"No, this must be a mistake," I said.

"What is?"

"This seat is taken."

"Is it?"

"It is."

She checked her ticket. "Oh yes, you're right. My seat is on the other side of you."

She stepped around my knees on her way to that seat. I looked the other way, but felt her staring at me.

"You look familiar," she said.

I shrugged, not knowing how to respond, or if this was some ploy to draw my attention to her. Meanwhile, someone in the row behind us tapped her shoulder, trying to hint that she should stop it, and no more chitchat, because the sounds of musicians tuning their instruments was already heard behind the scenes.

She licked her red lips and offered a gloved hand in a gesture that confused me. What are the proper manners here? Should I shake it or kiss it?

"My name," she said, "is Lana."

"Lenny," said I.

"Oh!" She touched a gloved finger to her forehead, and a sudden glint of recognition shot from the corner of her eye. "What a surprise! What a small world! Now I know who you are!"

"You do?"

"You're a marine, aren't you?"

"I am—"

"You're Ryan's friend, right?"

"You know Ryan?"

"I do! I'm his girlfriend, you must have heard about me, no? Anyway I got a letter from him, just the other day, with picture of both of you, looking so, so striking in uniform. You were standing there with those English girls all around you, in front of the embassy in London. Don't tell him I said this," she hissed in my ear, "because if you do I'll deny it, but you're even more handsome in person, especially in this fine suit, if you don't mind me saying so—"

"But I do!" said the man from behind.

And another one said, "Shush!"

She shrugged him off with a pretty smile, confident that no one can resist her charms, but she did lower her voice, just a bit.

"Talk about a coincidence," she said, crossing her legs and shifting position to cuddle up to me, as if she were my babe.

I left her question unanswered, because the house lights started dimming. To the sound of applause, which mixed with the sound of wind instruments from the orchestra pit, an announcer stepped out from behind the curtain and headed to the front edge of the stage.

Meanwhile, "Why are you here?" Lana went on to ask. "Is everyone coming home? I mean, has the war ended?"

There was a gasp from behind.

I said nothing to her, because nothing is something at which I am the best at saying, and because this was not the time to say a thing, especially not to someone who was so oblivious to what was going on in the world.

It maddened me to think that my friends were risking life and limb on the other side of the Atlantic Ocean and that civilian casualties were mounting all over Europe, only to be utterly ignored by the likes of this woman, whose only thought was finding someone, anyone to amuse her.

By now, the announcer came to a stand directly in front of us. "Tonight," he said, "we're proud to present a brilliant pianist whose lyrical sensitivity has been honed by acclaimed performances, in every concert hall all over the country, from Los Angeles to Boston."

I felt ignorant for not checking the program ahead of time, because of doubting that I would find myself in this place. I had no idea of what music to expect, nor did I know the names of the performers. Now my heart quickened with a sense of anticipation, which was as remarkable as the boredom that registered on Lana's face. I was surprised to see her subduing a yawn.

Meanwhile, the announcer went on. "If you haven't heard the name up to now," he said, "you've been missing out. Quite simply, this performer is known for an amazing virtuosity. One thing I can promise you: after tonight, you'll never forget her!"

Then he stepped back and cast a glance over his shoulder. With ghosts of light fluttering around its circle, the spotlight followed him, widening its focus as it went, until reaching the outline, the curvy outline of a grand piano. It washed the heavy, carved legs with light, then climbed over the Steinway and brought a figure standing by its side out of the shadows.

And there, against the background of richly decorated panels around the stage, in a long, shimmering evening gown that seemed to be aglow, was the one who had vanished, mysteriously, from my life. I looked at her bright, green eyes and for just a moment thought I felt her looking back at me.

No, I said to myself. From up there, she couldn't have spotted me. To her I am part of a crowd, a dark, anonymous mass with a glint here, a glint there, flashing across the glass of a pair of binoculars, aimed at her from this and that direction.

It was at that moment that by the pang, the sharp pang in my heart, I knew: love was not something I could decide not to do.

There I was, held by a spell.

Natasha.

Repose

Chapter 14

With a spring in his step, the announcer turned to Natasha and handed her the microphone. She brought it to her lips, but in her excitement could not speak at first, nor could she contain a smile.

"Natasha Horowitz," he said, to the sound of applause. "We're truly honored to have you here!"

"It's me who's honored," said Natasha, beaming broadly. "Playing at Carnegie Hall has been a dream of mine from early childhood."

"It's a dream for many musicians, but for you it's real," he said. "So now tell us, what will you be playing tonight?"

"This is a special piece for me," she said, "one that has been commissioned by Count Franz von Walsegg, an Austrian aristocrat who lived in Stuppach Castle. A lover of theatre, he was in touch with many composers, who agreed to deliver their works to him without revealing their identities, for which he paid them handsomely. This way he could retain sole ownership, and on occasion announce that the real composer was none other than himself."

"Really?"

"Really. Then, in 1791, following the death of his twenty-year-old wife, he commissioned a requiem mass from Wolfgang Amadeus Mozart."

"Please, share with us what this piece means to you," said the announcer. "What makes it special?"

"Oh, it's so stirring, and for many reasons," she said. "For the composer, what a grand gesture it must have been, creating this music for the repose of the soul of the dead!"

In a blink her words touched me. They reawakened the grief for my father. In his last days, his pain must have been crushingly strong. It must have prevented him from writing to me at full length. I felt him slipping farther and farther away from me.

I would never admit it to anyone, lest they think me an irrational fool, but closing my eyes I kept waiting for a whisper, a touch from beyond. I imagined him struggling, even now, to stay close. But other than the empty seat next to me, there was no sign, no presence.

I was grateful that at last, his flesh was free of suffering, but his soul, I sensed, was still troubled, as was mine. In different ways, this requiem was for both of us. We needed to find peace.

"Mozart wrote the composition on his deathbed. He never finished it," said Natasha. "I keep wondering how he might have brought it to completion, had he lived. Such is the riddle of this music. Such is the riddle of a premature departure."

I marveled at her words. She had lost her Pa not that long ago and understood, in the most profound way, what I was going through.

"And as for Count Franz von Walsegg," she went on to say, "he never remarried. Perhaps in his mind this music stood for eternal love, for faithfulness that persists, that carries what you feel across any and all boundaries, even in the face of death."

At hearing this I felt my heart hammering inside me. If the idea of faithfulness was one of the reasons for her choosing this piece, how then could she have deserted me? How could she balance such contradictions in herself?

As if she could hear my thoughts Natasha said, "And one more thing: contradictions! That's something I often think about, when it comes to this particular piece. It has it all: love, grief, deception. What a mystery we are, all of us, as you can realize thinking about the Count. Grieving for his beloved was painful, no doubt. Even so it never stopped him from mixing it with deception. He paid Mozart for the Requiem, intending to pass it off as his own."

"That," said the announcer, "may have been legal—"

"But not right."

"On a different note," he said, "I'm told that this piece was scored for basset horns, bassoons, trumpets, trombones, drums, violins, viola, cello, and organ. The vocal forces included soprano, contralto, tenor, and bass soloists, and of course a choir. But tonight, there's just you."

"Yes, just me. My late Pa transcribed it for piano four hands, and when I could no longer play it together with him—which happened months before he passed away—I transcribed it a different way, reducing it to just two hands."

"I can't wait to hear it."

"I can't wait to play it," she said. "Can't wait to bring you in, to hear the contrasts of this piece, its overwhelming contradictions."

With that Natasha handed the microphone back to him and curtsied to the audience. A wavy, red strand of hair slinked from her headband, which was decorated with delicate flowers, and glided over her bare shoulder. Below that, the bodice of her dress glinted as she turned around. And again, for just a second, I thought I felt her eyes fluttering in my direction, meeting my gaze. Everyone around me must have imagined that, too.

Natasha lifted the long, silky skirt of her dress, so its folds fanned out from the seam that hugged her hips. As she sat down they draped, full and flowing, over the piano bench, responding playfully to the light from above with a cherry red shine. A reflection of it lit her chin from below and lined the underside of her slender arms, just a touch. With a slow, deliberate motion she lifted her hand, letting it hover, for what seemed like the span of a thought, over its shadow over the keys.

Her fingers started flitting across the keys, and at once I was taken by the solemn, dramatic sounds she made rise over us. They came pressing against the far reaches of the hall, gathering ominously just below the vaulted ceiling, as if in preparation to blow it away and sweep us into the night. There was no repose for the soul, at least not yet. Instead there was something else, perhaps a sense of woe. It made me want to kneel down and surrender, give myself up to the unknown, to this darkness that was looming over me, over this entire space.

In a flash, the words *To You all flesh will come* flew into my mind. They brought everything I felt to a head: not only the sorrow that descended upon me during the last few days—ever since coming back to my father's empty place—but also pity, pity for the destruction and the waste I had seen overseas in recent months. Oh, and fear too, fear for the fate of us all, because in this war we suffered and made others suffer in return.

I closed my eyes. More words drifted before me as the music intensified, and now I realized where I must have seen them: the last thing my father had bought, perhaps together with tonight's tickets, was a record. I recalled seeing it on his desk and noting that it was still in its original, sealed cover. On the back, it quoted the lyrics from the requiem, translating their Latin phrases. *Day of wrath, day of anger... Will dissolve the world in ashes... That day of tears and mourning, when from the ashes shall arise, all humanity to be judged.*

In my hurry to put things in order I had given away all his records, including this one, which now I realized was a mistake. I should have kept it. Oh, was I in loss! Loss, I said to myself, glancing at the empty seat beside me. Loss.

Overwhelmed by it I felt, for the first time since my return, tears welling in my eyes. Sounds came washing over me, softening my soul, changing my pain into music.

By the end of her performance there was a long silence. Natasha came to the front and took a deep bow, which brought people to their feet, applauding her. The announcer came back onstage with a large bouquet of roses.

"From your admirers," he said, offering it to her.

She took it and gave the crowd a brilliant smile, but her face remained pale and her eyes—sad. Perhaps it was the impact of the music, still echoing inside her. The spotlight followed her as she turned back with a silky swoosh, then it dimmed.

A while later, curtains fell over the stage, sheer, translucent curtains through which I could still read an impression, a faint impression of her, exiting the stage.

The thought of leaping to my feet and running backstage to find her dressing room occurred to me, but I dismissed it. What was the point? Natasha gave me music, heavenly music that lifted me from my grief. I sat empty handed, with nothing to give back.

Meanwhile I glanced around at the audience. Everyone seemed to be in awe, all except the woman next to me. Why Lana was even here was a mystery. Music was not something she seemed to enjoy. I thought I remembered Ryan, my friend, mentioning to me that his girlfriend had tin ears, which at this point she signaled, without shame, by choking one yawn after another.

Reluctant to get up by herself, Lana clasped my arm with a pleading look, so I had no choice but to help her to her feet. Wobbling a bit over her high heels, she took a large, jeweled comb out of her purse and inserted it into her hair, which was extremely blond, to hold it in place, twisted up.

Then, with a little sigh, she told me how glad she was it was finally time for intermission, and she needed a man by her side, not someone who was stationed faraway, and who not only surrounded himself with English girls but also sent her pictures to boast about it, without any consideration for her feelings, and she wasn't jealous, really, but needed to be held, because what's a woman to do when she's lonely, and in particular she needed to be held by me, because right now she was a little tipsy, and would I accompany her as she headed for the bar.

Perhaps she figured I was not paying attention, because she concluded all that with, "Listen, Lenny. I need a drink. Would you buy me one?"

I hesitated. For months I ignored any and all temptations. I longed for my girl, but she was a star, and an illusive one at that. Too much time had elapsed since our one-and-only date, and even though I had just seen her onstage, standing right there in front of me, the distance remained.

She was unreachable.

A little devil awakened in my mind, suggesting that what had turned to ashes could never be rekindled. Natasha had forgotten me and knew nothing of my presence here. Call her a muse, an idea of love, an apparition. Call her anything but real.

Meanwhile, here was Lana, in the flesh. Without a doubt she was in heat, and she wanted me. Why, then, should I continue to deprive myself of pleasure? What was I waiting for?

Lana walked out of the auditorium ahead of me, swaying her hips in the most provocative manner, showing off a shapely leg through the slit in the back of her dress. And as if she could hear that hiss, the insistent hiss of the devil inside me, she cast me a flirtatious look over her shoulder.

By now we arrived at the intermission bar. We waited in line, and she ordered a martini. I paid for it.

Trying to act as if she were dainty, she touched a napkin to her glistening lips. The barmen poured a splash of gin and another splash of dry vermouth, stirred them together with ice, and strained the cocktail into a chilled glass, which he handed her.

"Ah!" said Lana, savoring the taste. "It's quite stiff!"

"As stiff as can be," said the barman, with a wink.

She took a greedy sip and offered me one, too. I refused.

Behind us, people started heading back to their seats, as the intermission was about to be over, but Lana was in no hurry to go back, and she told me so.

"The next performer is even worse than the previous one," she said, with a little hiccup. "I think it's someone quite old, and he's playing the violin, or something dreary like that."

"You don't like music, do you."

"I hate it with a passion."

"The tickets are expensive—"

"Not for me! I got mine as a gift."

"So did I."

"Perhaps we were meant to meet."

"Perhaps," I said, "we should go back to our seats."

"I'd rather not," said Lana. "Let's do something else."

"Like what?"

"Like going to my place."

I said nothing. Even so I knew I was on the verge of becoming reckless. Something naughty in me was listening to her with growing interest.

"Ryan wouldn't mind," she said. "After all, you're friends, right?"

"Yes," said I. "Friends we are."

"Kiss me, Lenny."

I said nothing again, and she knew better than to expect an answer. Without losing a beat Lana leaned over, setting her gloved elbows over my shoulders, combing playfully through my hair with one hand, holding her martini with the other. The aroma was intoxicating.

Then, before I could make up my mind what to do, she pressed her lips to mine, sealing them with yet another hiccup.

A few minutes later we stood outside the lobby of Carnegie Hall, shivering slightly in the cold wind. Snowflakes started swirling in the air. A taxi came around the corner with flashing lights and stopped for us some distance away, at the curb.

I dashed ahead and opened its door for Lana. She was still working her way in high heels, careful not to slip over the snow-covered areas, not to wobble too much. Waiting for her I spotted something: reflected in the top of the cab, between one snowflake and another was the sign of a flower shop. There it was, across the street, still open for business, despite the late hour and the chill.

I said to myself, roses!

Why didn't I think of it earlier, instead of idling about and complaining to myself about being empty-handed? I should have bought roses, dozens of them, for my girl. Perhaps it wasn't too late.

Lana uttered a little cry of surprise as I bolted across the street.

I dodged a car going this way and another one or two going the other way and then, breathless, handed the flower girl a few large bills, not even counting them. Bending over the round plastic buckets I swept bunches of roses into my arms.

And then, then—just as I was about to carry them across the street—I saw, over flutter of rosebuds, that the doors of Carnegie Hall were opening. Out marched a short, stocky figure, wrapped up to her ears in fur, with hair that was firmly fixed in place as if it were a hard, impenetrable helmet, thanks to the wonders of hairspray.

Behind her appeared a slender figure in a long wool coat. The hem of her cherry red skirt was barely visible under it. It floated just over the icy surface like a ribbon. I imagined it giving a silky swoosh.

"Wait!" called the girl. "Wait for me, Mamotchka!"

"Waiting, it's for losers," said her Mama in an impatient tone, as she crossed rapidly ahead of Lana, determined to catch that taxi.

"Hey stop!" cried Lana. "That cab is mine!"

"Not anymore," said the old woman, through tightly clenched teeth. "Quick, Natasha, let's go!"

By the time I cut in front of the cab, at the risk of being overrun by traffic, the girl had dutifully obeyed. Both of them were already seated inside, with the door closed and the engine starting to hum, but the window on Natasha's side was being rolled down. Perhaps she needed some air.

Without a second to catch my breath I threw myself onto the hood of the cab, dropping the flowers in a heap on top of it. Hoping that the old woman would not recognize me and that Natasha would, there I stood, panting, in an attempt to block the vehicle, somehow, from driving away.

Meanwhile Lana managed to arrive. She stamped her foot angrily and at once found herself plopped in an awkward position on the ice-cold pavement. From there, she glared at the old woman.

"Take the damn cab," she grumbled. "Who cares!"

And to Natasha, who seemed close to fainting, she said, "The flowers, they're mine!"

With that Lana rose, somehow, to her feet, ran to the hood, and gathered the roses I had spilled to her heart, looking at Natasha all the while.

"Better keep your hands off of them," she said. "And stay the hell away from my man, too!"

Natasha said not a word. Her Mama simply shrugged.

"Well? What are we waiting for?" she asked the driver, not expecting an answer. "Come on, hit the gas!"

With a screech, the taxi started swerving around me, shedding rose petals and frozen leaves as it went. Inside, the old woman clapped her hand to her forehead with a sudden gesture of recognition.

And as they drove off, she pointed at me, then wagged her forefinger, and with great menace, muttered, "You again!"

Until You're in My Arms

Chapter 15

Even before the taxi drove off, carrying Natasha away from me along with her Mama, I hailed another one. Dashing inside, "Quick!" I told the driver, as I pointed ahead. "Follow that car!"

Then, just before I had a chance to close the door, thump! Lana hopped in. With no apologies she landed in my lap, clutching what remained of the roses. She stuck her nose in one of them and sighed with misplaced gratitude.

"Oh what a lovely gesture!" she said. "Ryan never gave me flowers, not even on our first date, let alone on our anniversary, which happened the day he was drafted, so that to his relief, he had to miss it. He could learn a thing or two from you. My, what a gentleman, what a fine young man you are!"

I had not the heart to tell her that the flowers were not meant for her, exactly. The only thing I could do, as the car jerked into motion, was to ease her off of me.

"Oh, you don't have to tell me. I know," she said, with a sudden spark of intuition. "You bought them for that girl, that redhead! Don't say *no*."

I didn't.

"So cute, is what she is," said Lana, with a shrug. "So I understand, but I can't say I'm not jealous."

"You shouldn't be."

Smelling the roses and raising them to my nose, she asked, "What about these? Are they mine, now?"

"Sure," I said, as gallantly as I could, patting her hand over the broken stems. "You can have them."

"Oh," moaned Lana. "I would never have guessed it, looking at those muscles of yours. You have the most buttery touch."

"I do?"

"I'll make believe you meant to give me these flowers, if you don't mind."

"I don't."

For some reason she proceeded to tell me the whole story of how she had met Ryan. I could barely concentrate on it, because my mind was elsewhere. I was worrying that Natasha might slip away from me— this time forever—if the driver would fail to catch up to that cab.

Lana crossed one shapely leg over another, as if to pose for me, and went on with her account of things, which was becoming increasingly long-winded.

"A few months ago I went to a party," she said, in her Russian accent. "I made sure I arrived fashionably late —well, slightly later than that—because what's a girl to do if she wants to draw attention to herself?"

"Don't ask me."

Undeterred, she pressed on. "And as I entered, there he was," she said, "standing sheepishly next to his boss.

At the time he seemed like a shy, inexperienced young fellow, no, not his boss but Ryan himself, which may surprise you, because I can tell—looking at the pictures he has sent me from London—that nowadays he seems to be carrying on, with great confidence as well as vigor, with the ladies."

"Oh, forget them."

"Yeah. Drat those English ladies!"

"Amen," I said, absentmindedly.

"So to make a short story long," she droned on, "let me tell you about what happened at that party."

I tried, for her sake, to show some interest. "Can't wait to hear."

"His boss, a fatherly, middle-aged man, took me aside to tell me what a fine boy Ryan was, and if I asked him, which I didn't, we would make such a handsome couple, and perhaps, just perhaps, the most clever way to his heart was for me to show some familiarity with classical music, because Ryan was interested in it and was known to buy tickets, on a regular basis, for some God-awful concerts."

"How nice."

I was barely listening to her and must have missed a few sentences. Outside, an invisible hand started painting forests of frost upon the windowpane, through which I could see torrents of snow flowing towards us, lit by the headlights of our cab. I spotted patches of ice here and there and hoped we would not slide over them.

"Don't you worry," said the driver, glancing at me through the mirror over his head. "You're making me nervous, the way you bite your nails. Please, just sit back and relax, will you?"

Peering out of the one clear spot on my window, I told him to mind his own business, and my nails were mine to do with them as I please, and for heaven's sake not to lose sight of that taxi. It turned the corner, quite sharply, into a street just ahead of us.

I asked him, "Can't you drive faster?" only to be interrupted by Lana. "Don't you want me to continue?" she asked, this time with an indignant tone in her voice.

What choice did I have but to say, "Oh so sorry, please do."

"So by the next time I met Ryan," she said, "which happened a week or so later, I was much, much better prepared. Having done my homework I astounded him, really, by talking like a regular expert about *Tosca* and *La Boheme*, which I did in an incredibly casual manner and without even breaking a blush, as that would betray me. By the time I recited a few notes from *Madama Butterfly*, he was utterly impressed with me and even a bit enamored, to the point of buying concert tickets for both of us for an entire year, which was unfortunate and dreadfully boring, too."

"How nice."

"But he didn't bother to bring anything for me, not even a little token of attention, like flowers."

"How nice."

"I moved in with him shortly afterwards, and in exchange for him taking me to one dreary opera after another I taught him everything I knew, if you know what I mean."

"I'm sure I don't."

"But enough about me," she said. "Do you like my hair?"

I was tempted to counter with, "Isn't it part of you?" but instead just looked away.

"Oh," she sighed and moved on to something else. "Tonight's performance was no different than all the rest of them, just one yawn following another, but I think that this time I should thank him for it, because it gave me an opportunity to meet you!"

"When I go back to London I'll convey your gratitude to him."

With a nervous smile she said, "Oh, please don't."

Lana piled up a few more sentences, which I did not care to hear, after which she must have found herself out of breath and even worse, out of something to talk about, so at last there it was, a rare moment of silence, during which I could focus better on where the cab ahead of us was headed. It surprised me.

Up to this point I had expected Natasha and her Mama to be returning to their home in Summit, New Jersey, but after a few evasive maneuvers in a failed attempt to escape from us, their taxi turned around.

Now it drove back to the corner of Seventh Avenue and West 55th Street in midtown Manhatten, not far from where we had originally started. It stopped in front of the skyscraper. And there it was, the glitzy entrance to the Wellington Hotel, renowned for inviting its guests to "*explore everything there is to see and do in the Big Apple from our superb location near Broadway, Carnegie Hall, Central Park and Rockefeller Center.*" In countless ads, the place offered a guest-centered experience, whatever that meant, with the assurance that you would feel completely at home.

Still I wondered why home would not have been a better choice for them, given that it was familiar and contained everything they adored, all those pieces of gilded furniture which I could not put out of my mind since visiting Natasha, all those carved garlands of flowers and foliage, and those rosettes, shells, and urns. What's more, even though to me it looked like some palace in a foreign continent, to them it was home. I mean, there was no price tag on spending the night.

Our cab stopped with a screech. I leapt out and handed the fare to the cab driver, adding a few extra bills so he would bring Lana back to her place, wherever that might be. She refused. I insisted. He took the money. Off they went.

Meanwhile I saw Natasha getting out of that taxi and following her Mama into the hotel. Looking back over her shoulder, perhaps searching for someone, she hesitated for a just second before crossing the threshold. Her red hair, dotted with glittering snowflakes, was flapping wildly, unraveled by a gust of wind. Then the doors swung shut, cutting off my view of her.

I ran into the reception area, where a huge, spherical chandelier with myriad lights hung over the center of the space, directly over a round medallion design in the luxurious rug.

And there she was, turning to face me.

I was relieved to see that she was alone, at least for the moment, as her Mama was stomping off to the reception desk, there at the far end of the space, to get them a room for the night. It was an opportunity for us to talk, but we didn't. We couldn't.

Noting the most trivial details, such as flecks of snow turning to liquid on her wool coat, I stared at her, taking in the way she clasped one hand tightly with the other, the way her hair came spilling out of the headband. Setting a stark contrast to her pale face, one strand of hair cascaded down to her shoulder, like a river, aflame.

Natasha stared at me as if seeing a ghost.

Meanwhile in the background, a record started spinning, releasing sounds inscribed in its spiral groove into the air. Accented with intricate floral designs, the metallic horn of the gramophone projected toward us, letting out a cry. We knew it, knew the feeling.

I'll never feel joy again
Until you're in my arms
So lonely is my lane
Without your love, your charms

I figured I had to soften the tension between us. I had to speak out, and do it fast, in my smartest, most eloquent manner, and come up with something, anything that would make her want me back—but somehow I could not find the words.

My heart started hammering. Standing across from her I found myself, somehow, more isolated than ever. I was beset by anxiety, by rage that had been wrought by waiting, desperately waiting on the other side of the ocean months on end for a letter, a word from her.

All I could do was burst out with, "Why didn't you write to me?"

In turn she blurted out, "Why didn't you?"

Which set me back on my heels. I gasped, realizing that I should try to start this conversation over, this time in a gentler manner, without pointing blame. But it seemed to be too late. Not only silence stood between us now but also words.

"All these long months dragging by," said Natasha, "and not a word, not a sign of life from you! My God, I thought you were dead!"

"What? I wrote to you every week," I countered. "Sometimes a few times a week."

To which she cried, "No, that can't be! I never got a single letter."

"How can that be?"

"Are you doubting me, Lenny?"

"No, but—"

"But what, exactly?" she asked, flustered by the way I persisted with my resistance to her. "Every morning I asked Mama, as she went out shopping, to go to the post office, bring my fan mail and stuff, and send my letters to you. And then, when she came back, I would ask her, each and every time, if there was anything from you. Invariably, the answer would be the same."

"Let me guess! It was this: No."

She shook her head angrily, which brought a bit of color back to her cheeks. For a moment she was unable to utter a word.

"Natasha," I said, "anyone could have told you the answer even before the question was asked. Your Ma, she hates me—"

"Doesn't!"

"Does, too!"

"So?"

"So I bet it was her! She discarded my letters, or else she has them stashed somewhere, deep down in some dark corner, out of sight."

"No," said Natasha, shaking her head. "She's protective of me, but still. Ma would never do anything like that. I mean, I trust her. I rely on her, totally."

And a minute later she whispered, mostly to herself, "Would she?"

War Can Wait

Chapter 16

The old woman came back from the reception desk, with room keys dangling from her heavy hand. She pursed her lips with displeasure to see me standing next to her daughter. With a firm grip she pulled her away from me.

"Come, Natashinka," she said. "It's been a long night."

The girl responded with an intense look.

"You must be tired," said the old woman, spreading her fingers and raking the girl's hair so that every strand would be gathered up into the headband in the most proper way.

Natasha shook her head, but said not a word.

"Our room is ready," said her Mama. "Let's go."

The girl didn't stir.

On a whim, I stepped forward.

"I poured my heart into those letters, Natasha. Where they went, I have no idea. Somebody," I said, glancing sideways at her Ma, "somebody must know the answer to that!"

Face reddening, the old woman caught my gaze.

"Hello again, young man," she said, acidly. "Somebody must advise you to keep your day job, whatever that might be, because you're not going to make it as a writer."

"How would you know?" I asked, slyly. "Did you happen to read anything I wrote?"

She stammered. "I, I doubt that you've managed to write anything worth reading."

And to her daughter she said, in an urgent tone, "You coming?"

"In a minute," said the girl.

With a huff for an answer, the old woman turned around. She glared at me one more time, the keys in her fist clacking a furious rhythm. Then she marched off to wait for the girl at the opposite side of the reception area, in front of the elevators.

Natasha took a step closer and raised her head to me. I thought I spotted a little smile playing on her lips, which filled me with something potent, something I had not felt for quite a while: a sense of happiness.

The thought of sweeping her into my arms crossed my mind, followed by the thought of a kiss, but before I could make a move, here she was, hands gliding ever so tenderly over my shoulders. Then, closing her eyes, she turned her head away and clung to me in a sudden, unexpected caress, her cheek against my chest.

I stood there, utterly motionless, lost in the magic of her touch, my arms spread wide out, not daring to lock them around her. Somehow I sensed that by taking hold of Natasha I would risk her slipping away from me.

After a while I whispered, "Natashinka?"

She stepped back in surprise and said to me, "Don't call me that."

I asked, "Why not?"

And she said, "Because."

"Because what?"

"Only Ma calls me Natashinka. It moves me, and it does so in a special way. It's intimate. So I'm not ready for someone else—someone I barely know, and who is yet to gain my trust—to call me that."

"Today you're more careful than you used to be about me, and I think it's because of your Mama, what she thinks of me."

"You mustn't judge her."

"It's the other way around. She's judging me, judging my skills as well as my dream of becoming a writer."

"Ah," said Natasha, waving her hand. "Don't you mind that."

To which I said, "Can't help it. I do."

"Pa taught me how to play the piano. And Ma, she taught me never to be satisfied with how I do it. It's what she does."

I fell silent, which made her add, "If not for her, I wouldn't be searching for a fuller, more truthful expression of the notes."

"I shouldn't say anything," I muttered, "I know I shouldn't. But the way she meddles in my affairs, it isn't right."

"Please don't say that about her, Lenny. She simply wants to protect me."

"Not by violating me, us, and what I wrote to you! It was meant for your eyes only. I wasn't expecting someone else to open my letters and read them, let alone offer a literary critique!"

"I don't think she did it," said Natasha, and I noticed her casting a glance at the old woman, who started pacing impatiently back and forth and checking her watch.

"Then how, how d'you explain the way all those letters disappeared, both yours and mine?"

"You had no way of knowing this, Lenny, but when we lost our home, there was a big confusion, especially when we started to move from one hotel to another."

"What?" I cried. "You lost your house?"

She turned away. In profile, her lashes could be seen fluttering over a tear.

"We tried to keep up with my performance schedule," she said, "but without having a base, somewhere to call home, it was hard. So for a time, Ma neglected to ask the post office to hold our mail for us. I'm not sure why you didn't get my letters, but as for yours, they may have gotten lost in the shuffle, before she had a chance to sort things out."

"But I don't understand, how—"

"Not now. Ma is waiting for me. I have to go."

"But—"

"I'll tell you about all that happened, later."

"Later, when?"

"I have a free night tomorrow, no performances," she said, walking away. "Shall we meet here, same time?"

By now she was heading to the elevators. Below the hem of her wool coat, a ribbon of cherry red suggested the color of the dress. It was twirling, rolling about her with each footfall.

I matched my step to hers and softly I said, "We shall, Natashinka."

That night, back in my father's apartment, I took his white shirt off my back and peered into the darkness through the window, catching sight of myself. A reflection of me floated there, over the twinkling lights of the city. I closed my eyes and imagined myself flying. Then I imagined Natasha by my side, swifter than the wind.

No longer was I in the grip of loneliness. It had vanished, letting me welcome an unfamiliar mood. Boy, was I happy!

Yes, I was elated! Dancing like a madman around my mattress, which was the only thing here not yet sold, I asked myself what to do about the one problem I had, which was this: there were too many hours between now and the next evening, too many minutes to count down. I simply couldn't wait for my date.

Tomorrow, I whispered. Tomorrow.

Replaying in my mind what Natasha had told me I started parsing every sentence, examining every part in it this way and that, discovering new meanings in every turn of expression, every word. Again and again I heard her voice, saying, "When we lost our home, there was a big confusion..."

I recalled my visit to Summit, where she had lived then. Her house had been richly decorated and yet, there had been something about it that made it look not only in disrepair but also about to be deserted. The floor, covered with dust. The iron chandelier, missing half its light bulbs. Only now did I understand the reason for all that neglect.

As a result of her Pa's gambling habit, there must have been debts to pay and no money with which to do it. Then came the bills for his medical exams, and months later, his funeral.

Natasha must have known all along that she and her Ma would not remain there for long. They had been disengaging themselves from that place, while living there in a state of goodbye.

So now—despite her growing fame as a performer— she was homeless. Could anyone be successful and at the same time, poor? It seemed like a contradiction, something I had to work hard to resolve. With a shrug I decided that fact might be stranger than fiction.

I wondered, what happened to all that heavy furniture? The piano? The nicknacks? The rug? The pictures hanging over the mantle? How much of what they used to own had they salvaged? How much had they managed to carry away? Would these objects, these mementos of their days of grandeur, become a burden?

And now that they moved from one hotel to another, where would they store what they wanted to keep?

I asked myself, had the playing field between Natasha and me been leveled because of her misfortune? For months I had been saving most of my salary and could, perhaps, offer some help, once I figured out what she needed.

All of a sudden I sensed that there was a possibility, a real, practical possibility of contact between us. I relished the notion that if—by some miracle—she would accept my offer of support, her dear Mama would have to adjust. She would hate having to be on her best behavior with me, which would frustrate her. That in itself put an amused smile on my lips, giving me a jolt of cruel pleasure. Forced by gratitude, the old woman would have to realize, once and for all, that she could no longer afford to spite me. No more would she glare me down, muttering, "You again."

And as for Natasha, perhaps she was no longer as unreachable as she used to be. I sat down on the mattress, and intoxicated with hope I listened to the lullaby, coming faintly through the wall, as the neighbor sang her baby to sleep.

> Twinkle, twinkle little star
> How I wonder what you are
> Up above the world so high
> Like a diamond in the sky

The words were old. They were first published in 1806 by Jane Taylor in Rhymes of the Nursery and sung to the tune of the french melody dating back to 1761.

But there was something about them that held its power over me. To me, that star was none other than Natasha.

It was late. I looked around me. With the exception of the mattress, the apartment was empty. There was little left for me here. Up to now I had been planning to return to duty oversees as soon as things here were in order, which at last they were, but now I had a sudden change of heart. Maybe I could delay going back. After all, my leave would not expire for one more month. The story of my love was about to happen.

War could wait.

I looked at the walls that surrounded me, forming a blank shell of my past. Right here, next to the light switch, were dark smudges, layering one fingerprint upon another. I wondered, which ones were left by my father, which by me, reaching up high, sometime back in my childhood, to turn on the light?

And there, opposite me, my parent's wedding picture used to hang. In its place, a faint rectangle started to appear, as the wall paint all around it had darkened over the years. Everywhere I turned there were blank rectangles, marking the boundaries of missing picture frames, of old memories.

I imagined Natasha, back in Summit, New Jersey, casting a last glance at what used to be her place. The change I was undergoing was something she must have experienced not so long ago. For her—and for me, too— it was farewell to safety, farewell to what used to be home.

Make it One for the Heartbreak

Chapter 17

I had been paying no attention to my appearance lately, but in anticipation of tonight's date I could not afford to look like a slob. I had to prepare myself, so as to make the best possible impression on my girl. Aiming for a chance at a future with her, this I knew: together, we would be invincible. She would complete me.

Having lost my father I felt a void in me and yearned to fill it by starting a new family. This hope depended, first and foremost, on a good shave.

I set my shaving tools next to the sink: my badger brush, a bottle of Aqua Velva, and my cut throat razor.

Unfolded a small towel I soaked it in steaming hot water and pressed it against my face for a minute. Then I lifted the brush, its bristles tipped with silver, and used it to apply shaving cream to my chin. Around and around it swirled until the lather had formed into stiff peaks. I paused briefly to smile at my reflection, thinking that with that white, fluffy beard, it looked nothing like me. If Natasha could see me now, she would be smiling too.

I imagined us months, even years from now, a married couple repeating the same ritual every morning. It would never get old. She would be stretching my skin between her long, delicate fingers, the fingers of a pianist, until it was as tight as a drum. I would close my eyes, giving myself up to her.

She would angle the blade to my face and go through the first pass, traveling along the grain, shaving the stubble with short, rhythmic strokes, and finishing it off with long ones.

Then she would go through the final pass—the more dangerous one, when most accidents occur—this time, traveling against the grain.

I splashed some aftershave on my skin. On second thought I figured it might be a bit much. She might hate the smell. So I washed it off with soap and water, rubbing my face vigorously to make sure there was not a trace of it left, only to splash it all over again, just in case I was wrong. Yes, she might like it. No, perhaps not.

Oh God! So many hours to wait!

Next on my list was taking care of my father's shirt so it would feel fresh for tonight. I had washed it early that morning and hung it to dry on a hanger. Now I asked the next-door neighbor, a matronly, stout woman, to let me borrow her ironing board. There I stood, half-naked, squirting drops of water onto the collar, listening to them hiss and fizzle as I pressed the hot iron all the way around so as to loosen the bonds in the cotton fibers. There, no more wrinkles! The fabric straightened under my pressure and I knew it would hold its shape as it cooled.

All dressed up for my date I returned the board and asked the neighbor for the last item on my list, namely, recommendations for restaurants in the city. The one that stood out from the rest of them was a little brick saloon on Third Avenue that had opened its doors as far back as 1884.

"It's a great little place," said my neighbor. "And it has its own little quirks."

"Such as what?"

"Such as the human leg bones over the door."

"Really?" I asked, wondering if Natasha would appreciate such a morbid object, fearing that this in itself might ruin the promise of a romantic evening.

"Really," she said. "I think it's an Irish talisman of luck."

"Yes," I said, mostly to myself. "That's what I need, tonight of all nights. Luck!"

On the spur of the moment I decided to check out the restaurant ahead of time, just before picking up my girl. I grabbed my leather jacket and hopped aboard the Third Avenue El, an elevated railway in Manhatten and the Bronx, which was to remain in use until the Second Avenue Subway was built to replace it. Not so long ago, the *Third Avenue Elevated Noise Abatement Committee*, which consisted of men in the real estate business, claimed that the noise from the El constituted a menace to health, comfort and peaceable home life. I could not disagree with them more, especially on this particular, glorious day. The clinking and clanking of the train over the iron tracks was music to my ears.

Arriving at the corner of East 55th street and Third Avenue I recognized the building at once. It's name was designed to look like a signature of its original founder, *P.G. Clarke's,* drawn diagonally over a squiggly underline, using a fluid, white brushstroke that ran across the red bricks. Somehow it gave the place a personal touch.

Once inside I found myself ensconced in a vintage, old school atmosphere. The jukebox, which was coin-operated, played poignant love songs. The bar was separated from the dining room, to control the level of noise. Confident that Natasha would like this place for its classic New York feel I made reservations for us and turned to leave.

It was then that someone clapped me over the shoulder. He was a short, pudgy fellow who did not merit a second look, and even the first look was one too many, as the best part of him was a crumpled business suit, one that must have seen better days, sometime years ago.

Noting that I was not one of the regulars, he pointed out that there were little buttons in the walls from the prohibition era, to warn pub-goers that the police were on their way to bust them.

His voice rang familiar, but I could not be sure where I had met him until he talked again.

Raising his eyes to me, he uttered a cry of surprise. "Oh," he said, "don't I know you?"

To which I said, "Do you?"

"I think I do! Didn't you sit in the front row, just ahead of me last night, with that horribly talkative blond? I couldn't avoid but hearing her name. Lana, wasn't it?"

"Yes, it was."

"Oh God, couldn't you restrain that woman? She wouldn't shut up, not even for a moment, so when the show started I had to tap her over the shoulder, not once, not twice, but three times, simply to make her stop."

"We aren't together," I said, to avoid having to apologize for her.

"Sure you aren't," said he.

"Lana isn't my girlfriend," I insisted.

"Sure she isn't," said he.

And on second thought he added, "No matter. Don't I know it, women always complicate things, don't they?"

In turn I said, "If you say so. I'm not an expert in such things."

He introduced himself as Mr. Bliss, and said his name was somewhat misleading, or at least his clients would claim so, because they needed him only in times of trouble.

Mr. Bliss went on to say that he was about to expand his business as an attorney at law, perhaps even hire a secretary, just as soon as he could find some decent office space, and meanwhile he managed it single-handedly, out of some apartment in the South Bronx, and should I need his services—no need to say *no*, because you never knew, things could turn sour at any moment, even for me—so, in summary, should I need him, for anything really, here was his business card.

He stuck it in the pocket of my leather jacket, sat down at the antique mahogany bar, and invited me to join him by tapping the four-legged wooden stool next to him. I said, "No, I have to go."

His smile was moody. He glanced at me, with an unmistaken glint of admiration, and said, "Lucky you. You seem like you know where you're going."

"I do, tonight."

"How about one drink? It'll be on me. No? You're going to regret it! The bartender here is second to none. You're always able to catch his eye right when you need a refill. And he knows exactly when you want a glass of water without you ever asking."

Afraid that his sadness might rub on me if I stayed there any longer I said, "Thank you for the offer, but no. I can't be late. My girl is waiting."

Still, he pressed on. "This saloon, it's a magical place," he said. "Truly! Singer Johnny Mercer, you've heard about him, right? He sat right here a couple of months ago and penned a new song, just like that, on a napkin. It's going to be in the movies, I'm sure of it. It inspired me to write my own little version. No one but you will know about it, because who am I to be remembered?"

I shrugged, and he asked, bleakly, "Want to hear?"

"Perhaps another time," I said, walking away.

And from the corner of my eye I saw him going over to the jukebox, putting a coin in it and then, in a gesture of a salute, raising his empty beer mug to say goodbye to me and hello again to loneliness.

Midnight came and went

The place is empty, I'm so lonely and so spent

So fill my cup

And let me tell you, before my time's up

It's too late to give, she won't take

Nothing more to talk of

So make it one for the heartbreak

And one more for love

There was chill in the air, and a balmy breeze blew through 55th street as if to hurry me along. Not that I needed any urging. Before long I arrived at the Wellington Hotel. With a spring in my step I entered the reception area, then paced around the space, waiting for Natasha.

I wondered, what if her Ma would forbid her from going on a date with me? Even worse, what if she would insist on joining us, in the role of a chaperone?

So as soon as I saw both of them stepping out of the elevator I knew that my fears were not ungrounded.

I dashed forward, and feeling a bit embarrassed to kiss the girl while her Ma was there I did the next best thing. I took the old woman's hand and kissed it.

"Good evening, Mrs. Horowitz."

Pulling back her hand, "Not so good," she muttered. "Not with you drooling all over me."

But I could see that in spite of what she said, her face softened a bit.

"I made reservations for two, for a lovely restaurant, not too far from here," I said. "I wish I knew you were coming, because then I would have made reservations for you, too."

"Next time I'll be sure to let you know."

"Mrs. Horowitz, you've made me a happy man! I didn't dare to hope there would be a 'next time' but now that you mention it I know there would be! Let me kiss your hand again."

The old woman refused, but somehow she could not help smiling. Then she said, "I expect you'll bring my daughter back here, right after dinner."

"I will."

"I'll be waiting."

The girl kissed her wrinkled cheek and moved over to my side.

I glanced at Natasha. She wore a cashmere sweater blouse, which was part of a dress ensemble, the lining of the sweater matching the dress. It was crew-necked, wide at the shoulders and fitted around her thin waist, which emphasized her soft, rounded chest.

I tried not to gawk, because it made her look innocent and at the same time sexy, as if she were saying, "I'm a good girl," while at the same time, pointing out, "Look! I have breasts!"

I gave her a compliment for the lovely pattern of beads and sequins around the neckline, and her Mama was quick to step in-between us to mention that she herself had sawn these, with her own hands, which she started waving about for extra emphasis, and that the pattern was inspired by the work of a designer named Claire Potter, who included decorated evening sweaters in her collection, which you could see for yourself in every fashion magazine, and that no one could tell, no one could guess that what her daughter was wearing was not part of it, and by *a part of it* she meant the collection, not the magazine.

"How lovely," I said.

And the girl said, "Thank you, Mamushka."

Then we rushed out together, leaving the old woman behind us.

"Couldn't wait to see you," I told Natasha. From her blush I knew that she couldn't wait, either.

I extended my arm to her, and she put her hand in mine. Her touch was all I could feel, all I could think about. The heat between the palms of our hands made the chill in the air melt away. At long last, we were joined.

When It's Her You Embrace

Chapter 18

The bar was crowded when we arrived, and so was the dining area. Our table was smack in the middle of it. Light bounced playfully over the ringlets of her auburn hair as she sat down. Far behind her, a red brick wall served as a backdrop, upon which a rustic, slotted wooden box—marked *Suggestions, Complaints, and Compliments*—was fixed. Left and right of it hung scores of framed, signed photographs. Looking at them you would discover the faces of some of the more famous among the regulars, such as Frank Sinatra.

"Wow," said Natasha. "What an exciting place!"

And I said, "I wish I had a camera to take your picture. One day it'll hang on the wall up there, and everyone will know what a great pianist you are, and how the audience adores you!"

Meanwhile, a familiar voice behind me asked for the bill. I cast a look over my shoulder and saw a crumpled suit. There was Mr. Bliss, sitting alone back there, in the corner. The last thing I needed was for him to distract me by starting a conversation or giving me unasked for lawyerly advice. I slumped in my chair, hoping he would not spot me. My only relief was knowing that he was just about to leave.

All the while, the enticing smell of bread wafted in the air. It reminded me that I had not eaten all day, had not even thought of food. At first Natasha said she didn't want anything except for a small appetizer, perhaps because she had noticed the prices on the menu.

But when my order of creamy tomato soup arrived, along with a farmstead cheddar toast, the fragrance was so pleasant that both of us leaned over to take it in. We ended up sharing it, our tablespoons sliding playfully over each other down there, at the bottom of the bowl. If not for table manners I would have stuck my face in it and licked it clean.

"Boy," I said. "Am I hungry for more!"

And she said, "So am I."

Having passed next to us on his way out Mr. Bliss gave me a wink behind her back. "One day a blond," he said in a gruff voice, to no one in particular, "the next —a redhead! How lucky can a guy be?"

Natasha must have sensed something going on between him and me, because she raised an eyebrow.

After a while she asked, "You know that fellow?"

"Barely," I said, "but I think I remember him. He sat in the second row behind me, at your performance last night at Carnegie Hall."

"Why, then, is he talking to you?"

"Is he, really? I haven't been paying attention. What was it he said?"

She gave no answer, except for lowering her eyes over a glint of distrust.

I wondered then if she had recognized me yesterday in the audience, even though it was unlikely. After all, I had been in the dark and she—in the spotlight. Had she noticed Lana sitting next to me? Did she suspect that I had taken her to the show?

Natasha started tapping her fingers on the checkered red-and-white tablecloth, to the sound of a melody that seeped in, somewhat faintly, from the direction of the bar.

> I am trying so hard to hold back my tears
> I've hoped you'd be mine for all future years
> How can I believe you, how can I trust
> When you're with her, ignore it I must

Over the reverberation of the song I asked her, "D'you know who accompanied me to the theatre?"

She shook her head, No, with a tired expression that suggested, "Spare me your lies."

I said, "Truly, Natasha, I was there with my father."

And she said, "Ha! The only one by your side was that woman."

"No," I countered. "She was nobody I knew. Just a stranger."

She looked up at the ceiling, rejecting me, listening.

> All that you give me are those empty vows

Only hurt and suspicion is what you arouse

My heart is breaking when it's her you embrace

She's in your arms, it should be my place

"Let me explain," I said. "My father, he bought the tickets for himself and for me, just before he passed away, a little over a month ago."

"Oh my God, Lenny, I didn't know. So sorry to hear it."

"That's why I came back to the States, hoping to see him, hoping to say goodbye."

"Oh," she said, with a sudden sense of insight. "Now I understand! His was the empty seat by your side."

"Yes," I said. "It was."

Natasha placed her hand over mine, and for a while we stayed silent. I hoped that words would not cut into the moment, into the warmth of us.

Our waiter was happy to suggest dishes that were a staple of the saloon, which was all about comfort food, such as burgers and mashed potatoes. Natasha asked him about *onion strings*, as she had never heard of these before, and he went into a detailed explanation.

"First," he said, "you must slice the onions quite thinly, which requires a sharp knife and a steady hand. Second, you must soak the slices in buttermilk—with a bit of flour, a dash of salt, and a bit of pepper—for at least an hour before frying. Third, you must ensure the oil is at the right temperature before throwing in the strings."

"Sounds great," said Natasha.

A little while later he came back, carrying our plates. The burgers were perfectly seasoned, the onion strings were crispy, and the side dish of melt-in-your-mouth mashed potatoes was simply delicious.

We ate. We talked. We laughed.

Then, waiting for our chocolate fudge brownie sundae to arrive, I thought I was too stuffed to handle even one more bite. Natasha suggested we ask for the bill and forget about dessert, only to change her mind upon seeing it: a warm brownie topped with cool, creamy vanilla ice cream, drenched with drizzle upon drizzle of chocolate syrup. It was so tempting that in a snap, both of us became hungry all over again.

When we finally got out of the saloon, the night was cold. I noticed that she was trembling, so I took the leather jacket off my back and wrapped it, ever so tenderly, around her shoulders. And at once, something came over me. I could not help but brush my fingers along the delicate line of her neck, plunging them into the thick of her hair. I breathed her flesh, pulling her closer.

Natasha clung to me and I gathered her, this time fiercely, into my arms, feeling her nipples harden through the knit blouse, losing myself in the taste of her lips, in the shiver, which was not hers anymore but ours, hoping the moment would never end. And as it was happening I already knew I would never forget it.

Here it was, the essence of sweet.

Then she separated from me. I looked at her eyes, begging her—without saying a single word—to come back into my arms, but we both knew that alas, it was time to go. We started walking back to the hotel. Along the way passers-by turned to look at us.

"Look at that handsome couple!" said one.

"She's so beautiful," said another.

And a third one said, "Look at him, how serious he is."

Once the crowd thinned out Natasha said, "So just like me, you too are going through a change."

"I am."

"For me, it feels as if I've been expelled not only from a physical building but also from my past, from my childhood."

"Don't I know it! It's hard to think that someone else is taking your place."

"I miss home. I miss every little thing, every object in it, because it reminds me of what happened, of little tokens of affection that come back to me, like the crystal vase, which Pa brought for Ma nearly ten years ago to mark their anniversary."

"When I came to Summit for our first date I saw it, set there on the dining room table."

"It used to capture the light so brilliantly, Lenny! I used to put fresh flowers in it every Friday. D'you know the secret of a perfect arrangement?"

"Tell me."

"It's the spiral, where each new stem is slanted against the previous one. I would choose the best and biggest bloom for the center and arrange the other flowers at an angle around it, mixing the shades of white, pink, and purple and creating a wonderful dome of flowers."

"Oh, Natasha, I can just imagine it."

"Then I would stand back and enjoy looking at it, thinking what a beautiful painting it would make, with the lovely shapes of orchids, spray roses and Asiatic lilies brushed upon the canvas."

"What would you call it?"

"Still life, with memories."

"I know how you must feel," I said, thinking that the vase, which used to be a solid object in which to hold stems, was now given to the fluidity of the mind.

"Yes," said Natasha, as if she could hear my thoughts. "Soon that vase will be forgotten. It'll cease to exist."

"But then, new memories will be formed."

"A lot has happened to me during these last months, and a lot has happened to you too, Lenny. I have so much to tell you, and so little time."

I smiled at her, thinking that the most important thing—our love—was still a story waiting to happen.

As the Wellington hotel came into view, she stopped in place all of a sudden and said to me, "I don't know where I'll be a week from now. Ma said we can't afford staying here anymore."

"You can't disappear from my life again," I said. "I won't let you."

"I have no power over it, Lenny This is a tough time."

"Then, let me make it easier for you."

"You can't."

"Perhaps I can."

She raised her eyes to me as if to ask, how?

And I said, "My father's apartment is ready for a move-in. By now I've emptied it of all his stuff. The rent is paid for the next six months, my father made sure of that, so it would be a pity to let it go to waste."

The last sentence was somewhat of an exaggeration. Rent was paid for only through the end of this month, but I figured that a little white lie would make it easier for her to accept what I had to offer, so I went on with it.

I asked, "How about you and your Ma moving into the place, at least for a while, until you come up with better plans?"

She was speechless for a moment.

Then she said, "Wow," followed a minute later by, "And where would you live?"

To which I replied, "In a month from now I'll have to go back to England, anyhow. Until then, I'll figure something out. Perhaps I'll ask Uncle Shmeel if he'll let me sleep on his sofa."

For a while she considered the offer.

At last she said, "Ma would never agree. I know her. She's too proud to accept a handout, especially from you."

"Why don't you ask her," I suggested. "No need to refuse me in her name, right? And who knows, maybe she'll surprise you!"

"I doubt it," said the girl, "even though necessity has a way of humbling us. We do need a place, somewhere to call home."

She ran into the reception area, and just before the doors closed behind her I called out, "Natasha! When will I see you again?"

And through the glass, her lips formed the most marvelous word in the world.

"Tomorrow."

The Wind that Wrapped Us in a Chill

Chapter 19

The next morning, I woke up to the sound of a song, playing from the radio on the other side of the wall, in the neighbor's apartment:

> That night in the city we heard the big heartbeat
> We felt it go through us every step, every street
> The glitz that spelled a thrill
> The stars that rolled and spun
> The winter wind that wrapped us in a chill
> And forged us into one

The song was perfect for evoking the feel of last night's date with Natasha. It filled me with joy, but also with worry: I cared deeply about her and could not bear the thought of her moving from one place to another, like a gypsy.

With all my heart I hoped that she would agree to move into my father's apartment and make it her home. But what if she would refuse? Then, in all probability, I would lose contact with her upon my return to London.

I feared this outcome. I dreaded the moment when our story would be cut off.

To move things along in the right direction I spent the entire morning preparing the place for the possibility of handing over the keys to her. First I used a large sponge and a solution of water mixed with a few drops of dishwashing liquid to remove dust and grease. Then I taped the trim with masking tape and used the roller, which was an ingenious painting device, invented only last year.

And a strange thing happened while I was rolling paint over the walls: with every stroke I felt as if I were whitewashing the traces of my family, of guests and neighbors who had visited us during holidays, birthdays, parties, even wakes. The fingerprints all of them had left behind were now lost to sight. I felt as if it were my own shadow that I was blotting out, my own existence.

No longer did I belong here.

And I asked myself: moving on, how would I preserve the past? Clearly I could not rely on physical mementos, on objects and houses, to remain in place so they could hint at history. What would help me recall events in my life and in the lives of others?

Perhaps I could put pen to paper and capture some of the stories I had heard. Then, these stories would live forever. The characters would leap from my mind onto the paper, and from there—into the mind of readers everywhere.

Where would I start? With something that happened in my early childhood? Or else, something that happened this year? After all, these last months turned out to be simply amazing. I was lucky, and so grateful, to come across such remarkable characters. How would I go about depicting them?

For some time now I had a vague wish to become an author, but had no real experience with the craft of writing. After all I had never written a story, never felt the urge to do so, until now.

With paint-stained fingers I opened my little notebook, only to find out that even a blank page could have an expression. This one, to me, seemed rather intimidating.

The first idea that came to mind was to write about my girl. I started a sentence and immediately stopped. This story had no end and no middle either. It would be hard for me to develop it, having only a beginning.

Besides, Natasha was too close to me, close to my heart. My passion for her blinded me. I needed someone else to write about, someone I could examine at some distance, so as to describe him in an objective manner, seeing into his heart and guts, the way I believed a writer would do.

My next idea was to write the story of one of the fellow marines I had come to know, like Ryan. Our conversations gave me plenty of material, and whatever details I missed I could fill in from my own experience. One thing that intrigued me about him was the contrast between the way he saw himself and the way his girlfriend, Lana, saw him. It was a conflict in the making, wrapped up in the guise of an affair.

I remembered him telling me, "So many cute babes here, and they all adore us and want to have a little chat, which is a bit hard to understand, because they speak with that fascinating, mind-bending foreign accent, which makes me forget the name of my girlfriend back home."

And I recalled Lana saying, "At the time he seemed like a shy, inexperienced young fellow, no, not his boss but Ryan himself, which may surprise you, because I can tell—looking at the pictures he has sent me from London—that nowadays he seems to be carrying on, with great confidence as well as vigor, with the ladies."

It was then that I came up with the brilliant idea of writing their story, with shades of deceit on her part and infidelity on his. I would develop it in stark contrast to our love.

Having worked all this in my mind, the first sentence came to me with surprising ease:

Ryan was first introduced to Lana at his boss's house, where he and a few other guests had to stand around waiting for dinner, with nothing but some dry nibbles to help pass the time, and nothing but the weather to keep the conversation afloat—until a full hour later, when she finally arrived.[6]

---

[6] This story, eventually titled *Leonard and Lana,* is included in full in the novel Apart from Love

I could easily describe how my character would become infatuated with Lana. After all, I was a man in love:

He was seated at the table next to her, and noticed her long, wavy hair. It had blond streaks, and smelled good. The perfume was very subtle—just enough to put him under a spell.

Then I asked myself if Ryan would object to me writing about him. Would I be invading his privacy by doing so? Should I change the name of my character to protect the innocent? I decided against it, at least for now. After all, if you could not annoy somebody, there was little point in writing.

Her wrist was so close to his that he could sense her warmth through the fabric of her blouse, and it set him afire. By the end of the main course he managed to ask her, with a sudden catch in his voice, to pass the butter. The effort left him speechless, and so he thanked her in his own manner, with a slight nod but without meeting her eyes.

All of a sudden I discovered that there was little time to complete the story. I had to hurry, remove the masking tape from the trim, place the paint bucket and painting tools in storage, finish cleaning up the apartment, wash the stains of both paint and ink from my fingers, and get ready for my date.

My last task was to carry the old mattress out into the street. I would not be sleeping in this place tonight. Uncle Shmeel had already agreed to let me use his sofa.

I shined my shoes, dressed up and opened the door to leave, but felt compelled to come back in and cast a last look. While at it I gave in to temptation and scribbled one more paragraph in my story. In it I began to give my character some of my own traits, such as the love of music. I figured it would help me breathe life into him.

And even though his name on paper was still Ryan I began to think I should change it. He was a creature born out of my own mind, and needed a name that reflected it.

Perhaps, Leonard.

I crossed out a few words, rearranged a couple of sentences, and read the paragraph out loud, so I might hear the sound of it:

Leonard discovered that—just like him—she loved Opera. With a sudden blush, Lana told him that she could appreciate the purity of vocal tone. She said she adored Puccini and could even describe, in a heavy Russian accent, several passages from the greatest Italian operas written by him. Her cheeks were so red, so rosy! She talked about Tosca, about La Boheme, and by the time she recited a few notes from Madama Butterfly, Leonard knew he had to have this woman, even though the color of her eyes was still a mystery to him.

The song started playing again. This would be the last time I would hear the radio here, on the other side of the wall. I left the place, thinking, Manhattan, here I come!

I Pine for You, Day and Night

Chapter 20

Later that evening, I entered the reception area of the Wellington Hotel with a craving that could not be satiated, at least not yet. In my hands I carried a little box of chocolates, which I had bought for my girl on a whim, an hour earlier at *Altmann & Kühne*.

Established two years ago at Fifth Avenue, the confectionery had recently been purchased by an American investor, but continued operating under the Austrian brand, which was highly prestigious. Natasha would surely recognize it and delight in the quality of its handmade chocolates and bonbons.

Love was in the air. I sensed it all around me. A record was spinning around on the gramophone, releasing one touching note after another, making me ache with desire.

Dark or light, deep in this heart of mine

There's a crazy beat pounding 'cause oh, just for you I pine

And its agony won't be through

Till you let me give myself, give all of me to you

I pine for you, dark or light

At the far end, the elevator doors opened. I thought of dashing over there to surprise Natasha. Instead I ended up taking a step back, because out came her Mama.

Mrs. Horowitz locked eyes with me at once, and it took all my concentration not to take another step back.

She clomped in my direction, then plonked herself down on the oversized couch that stood on one side of the elegant rug. Waving her hand at me in a commanding gesture, she pointed at the matching couch that stood on the opposite side.

"You," she said. "Sit down. We need to talk."

"Where's Natasha?" I asked.

"She'll be down shortly," said her Ma. "Now sit."

I did.

Narrowing her eyes, she leaned over to ask, "What's that thing you're holding?"

I rose to my feet and passed the box to her. Wrapped in beautiful paper, it was an artwork in its own right, designed to look like a miniature chest of drawers, in which sweets were stored.

The woman licked her colorless, wrinkled lips, and turned the thing over and over, examining it carefully under the lights of the huge chandelier. At last she returned the box to me, somewhat unwillingly, as if she hated to part with it.

"So," she said. "Maybe I've misjudged you."

I looked at her in surprise.

"Really, Mrs. Horowitz?"

"I said, Maybe."

"Never mind about me. Have you given any thought to my offer? Natasha has told you about it, hasn't she?"

"She has, but I'd like to hear it directly from you."

"Take it as an invitation: the two of you can move into my father's apartment, as soon as you like, and at no expense to you, make it your new home."

Leaning forward on her elbow and cupping all three of her chins in her hand, the old woman studied me at great length. At last she said, "It's more generous than anyone can imagine, to the point that it makes me wonder."

"About what?"

"About your wisdom, naturally! Because if you're clever then I must worry about your intentions, and if you're not, then I must worry why Natasha would fall in love with such a nincompoop. Either way I must protect her."

"Protect her you must, and the best way to do it is by making sure she is in a safe place."

She kept looking at me searchingly over the rim of her glasses, as if she could not put full trust in the optical lenses when it came to studying an unusual scientific specimen such as me.

Growing tired of it I said. "Well? Don't make me beg. Will you accept my offer?"

"Maybe," she said a third time, still reluctant to commit.

"I see," said I. "This is a definite possibility."

"What I can say at this point is this: I'm somewhat more willing than before to get to know you, young man, not only because of this chocolate box, and not only because of your offer, but most of all because—contrary to all expectations—you keep coming back, time and again."

"So you respect how persistent I am?"

"More precisely, I hate it."

To which I said, simply, "Mrs. Horowitz, I love your daughter."

She raised an eyebrow, but avoided the temptation to poke fun at a poor suitor. Instead she turned her attention to practical matters.

"So now, let me understand in more detail," she said. "The rent is paid?"

"For six months."

"And the place is ready?"

"Yes. This morning I threw the old mattress away. It was the last thing there. And I painted the place. It's clean and fresh."

In a flash, I imagined the fancy, carved furniture Mrs. Horowitz would acquire anew to bring in, all those Russian accents and the gilded frames and knickknacks, all of which would create a mini-palace of sorts. At the thought of it, a smile escaped my lips.

In turn, she gave me a severe look.

"One thing must be clear between us," she said, wagging a finger at me. "This is not to be treated as a handout. If we take you on your offer, it's going to be nothing more than a business arrangement."

"Of course, Mrs. Horowitz."

"I'm going to pay you back every penny, and that's a promise you can take to the bank."

"No need for formalities, Mrs. Horowitz."

"We're going to treat this not as a favor, but as a loan. Do we have an understanding?"

"Yes. We do."

"When will you vacate the premises?"

"I already did. And I've brought the key with me, Mrs. Horowitz. You can have it."

I fumbled in my pocket, took out the key, and presented it to her. She took it. And as it exchanged hands, Natasha came out of the elevator. She was wearing a scarlet sweater blouse with a soft bow at the neck, and a black skirt that played out her delicate curves.

At once, the conversation changed its tone.

"Mama," said the girl, as she approached. "Did Lenny tell you of his plans? After his military service, he's going to become a writer!"

The old woman pursed her lips, but not before letting out a heartfelt sigh. "Oy Vey."

"Yes," I said. "That's my dream. And it was inspired by something Natasha wrote to me, almost a year a go, in her first letter."

"I did? Really?" asked the girl.

"Really. Don't you remember?"

"No, what?"

"You said, '*I enjoyed your stories and would love to read more of them. Your words touched something in me... You, Lenny, you should become a writer.*'"

"Oh, I forgot about that. But I do remember your first letter."

Before I could come clean about it and explain that it was the only one of my letters that was not written by me, but rather by my friend Aaron, Natasha added, "It was brilliant."

I felt my face reddening as I said, "Brilliant it was."

The old woman cut in. "Listen here, Dostoyevsky," she said. "The only privilege of being a writer is a dubious one: you have the freedom to starve anywhere."

"I'm sure you're mistaken, Mrs. Horowitz. I can make a living at it."

She threw her hands up in the air. "Didn't your father teach you anything? There's something you must do before you start relying on your scribbles to make ends meet."

"What's that?"

"First and foremost you must acquire an education, which is to say, a professional degree, so that you'd be able to get a decent paying job, without which no self-respecting girl will seriously consider marrying you."

She glanced at her daughter, while holding a hand up to prevent her from responding. Natasha said nothing. Instead she bit her lip.

Meanwhile, the old woman pressed on. "All those courses at the university, they're not a complete waste of time, even if at present you may think they are. They'll serve you well, not only to earn a living but also to sharpen your skills as a writer. You may learn a thing or two from them, young man."

"Like what?"

"Like, when expressing thoughts, one should never generalize."

I considered mentioning that she had just generalized about never doing so, but on second thought decided to think twice about it.

So I asked, "What else?"

And she said, "The passive voice is to be avoided."

I took out my pocket notebook and wrote it down. "Just listening to you, Mrs. Horowitz, I'm getting better at my craft. Any more advice?"

"Yes. Avoid clichés like the plague."

"I'm making a note of it."

"Good," she said. "Last but not least, avoid overuse of rhetorical questions. Know what I mean?"

"No, not exactly," said I. "But one of these days I'll figure it out, I think."

The old woman leaned into her thick feet and with effort, got up.

"Now I have to go," she said. "I have an appointment with the stage manager. There are some urgent negotiations that need to be finalized before Natasha's next performance. Let me leave you with one last thought."

Natasha and I looked at each other, then at her.

"Well?" I said. "What is it?"

Mrs. Horowitz answered by asking, "You're going back to London in less than a month, right?"

"Yes," I said. "I have to. My leave is about to expire."

"And there's a war going on there, isn't there, right?"

"There is, all over Europe."

"Don't I know it. It's been a long time, ever since the Battle of France, since we got a letter from my nieces, the Rosenblatt sisters. Last I heard they were working in some nightclub in Paris. I hope nothing bad has happened to them." She paused for a minute and went back to her line of questioning. "So, young man, casualties are mounting?"

"They are," I said, not quite knowing where she was heading with all that.

"So," she said, "in Heaven's name, don't get married."

"Mama—"

"Mrs. Horowitz—"

"Hear me out," she said, this time even more firmly than before. "The last thing I would wish for my daughter is to become a war widow, Heaven forbid. You wouldn't want that for her either, young man, would you?"

I hung my head between my shoulders and shook it, No.

In a triumphant tone of voice, "Wait for the end of the war," she told me. And to Natasha she said, "Wait for his safe return, will you?"

Natasha said nothing, and the old woman turned to go. "And by the way," she said, this time to both of us, "the two of you are practically strangers. It won't hurt to get to know each other, in the little time you have left, before jumping into marital bliss. Trust me, it's not all that it's cracked up to be."

With that, she wrapped herself up in her fur coat, gave us a nod over the raised collar, and out into the street she went. We saw an impression of her stout figure through the glass, then the outline of a cab stopping for her, and then nothing too clear, except flashes of car headlights shining through.

"Would you like to go out for dinner?" I asked Natasha.

"Oh," she said, in place of an answer. "I think I forgot my coat upstairs."

"Let's go get it."

I noted the set of suitcases, ready to be carried away the next day, standing by the side of the door. Natasha unlocked it. Crossing the threshold she hinted at the other door, the one at the opposite end of the corridor, which led into her Ma's room.

"Mama's right," she said. "She always is, and it drives me crazy."

I waited outside, expecting her to get in just long enough to pick up her coat. Instead, Natasha took her time. I heard the sound of water running in the faucet, then the rattle of a drawer, opening and closing, and a brief rustle of paper.

At last she called out to me, "Lenny! Come in, there's something I want you to have."

I entered. The decor overwhelmed me with elegance. There was a regal chandelier in the center of the room and two table lamps, one on each side of her bed, with oatmeal-colored, bell-shaped shades and a gilded, antique finish that accentuated the detailing of their bases. One of them was lit. It shed soft light over the pattern of the wallpaper and over the curve of the carved headboard. And that bed!

Oh, I could not even begin to describe it. This was beyond pillows and sheets. It was an ensemble, the likes of which I had never seen before, a symphony of shapes and designs in gold and deep purple. I thought I would never disrupt it by touching this bed, let alone sleeping in it. Somehow it would make me uneasy. Natasha hopped right into the middle of it.

Oh God, I thought. After living in such elegant surroundings she would not stay in my father's apartment for long. As a soldier I could not provide for such extravagance.

"Take off your jacket," said Natasha.

"What?" I asked.

"Give it to me."

I did.

She took the leather jacket, laid it by her side, found the pocket, took out the little notebook, and started inserting a long, perfumed envelope into it.

"What's this?" I asked.

And she said, "Just something I wrote. I want you to have it. Something to remember me by when you go back to London."

I dropped to one knee at the side of the bed and raised my eyes to her, watching her long fingers as they smoothed over the flap of the envelope to make sure it was sealed.

"Let me read it, then," I said.

"Oh no, Lenny. Not now."

"At least, give me a little hint, Natashinka. Tell me what it's all about."

She blushed. Then she touched her cheek, trying to calm herself down, because now she was blushing over having blushed before. Meanwhile I noticed the silky fabric of her camisole. The edge of it came into view briefly, peeping out under the scarlet bow, right here at the lip of her sweater blouse. Then it disappeared.

At last she said, "It's a page from my diary. It's where I record my thoughts."

"Is it about last night?"

"Oh no. It's about the first time we met."

I was moved, and told her so. Her eyes widened as I took the notebook out of the pocket of my jacket and opened it to look at the envelope. On the back side of it there were only two letters, N for Natasha, L for Lenny. They were drawn together in a fancy pen stroke. I touched my lips to it and put the envelope back in place without losing a beat and without trying to pry it open.

"I shall save it for later," I said.

"And for always," said she.

"Yes," I promised. "For always."

Natasha smiled, bouncing happily between one pillow and another. Wave after wave, her hair unfurled around face, her neck. She turned over to lie on her belly, swinging her feet back and forth in the air.

"Here, I brought you a little something," I said, presenting the chocolate box I had bought for her.

She found it charming. I opened it. Inside were Liliput confections in red, pink, green, and black, each one hand-made: whipped, rolled, filled and ornamented. We looked at each other, wishing to surrender to temptation and at the same time trying to resist it, because at first glance, these sweets were too precious to eat. But this craving was stronger than both of us, and the only question was, would she yield to it before I did?

And another thing: how long could I hold myself back from making love to her?

Natasha leaned closer to me with a playful glint in her eye and reached over to pick a miniature chocolate ball, which she let melt on her tongue. She gave away a little moan, as if her delight came from the gut and couldn't be expressed in mere words. Now I could see not only the edge of her camisole, which cast a lacy shadow over her skin, but also one of her breasts, all the way down to the hard nipple.

Out of excitement I rose to my feet and with a single thrust, tore the comforter away. It dropped to the floor behind me. Natasha rolled away to the other side of the bed, her sweater blouse loosening off one shoulder.

Then she came back to hold out a chocolate-covered marzipan ball before me, so I might bite into it.

Instead I kissed her fingers, relishing the taste.

In her pleasure she could not help but utter a little sigh and let go of the delicacy. Slightly melted, it slipped from her hand onto the sheet, leaving a dark, aromatic stain.

"Have another one," she murmured, eyes closed.

"It's you I want," I whispered, ever so softly, in her ear.

From there I explored her, stroke by stoke, from the long line of her neck down to her waist and around the mound of her hips, as if she were a landscape with hills and molten rock: quiet in some areas, explosive in others. When I reached the valley she erupted in a cry. I drew her into my arms, my body coming and going of its own accord. I felt her legs parting before me as I hardened, then closing together, knees rising, pressing against my groin as she tried to deny herself, deny her own arousal.

At one point I thought of letting go of her, or at least delaying the moment of release, only to find her clinging to me anew, with a wild, desperate quiver of the flesh. And before either one of us knew what we were doing I happened across that sweet spot, where she was turning to liquid.

I could not even recall, later, if I had unzipped her skirt or if she had done it herself. All I knew was that after all these months of being away, imagining her touch, feeling our first kiss fade away into a distant memory, at last here we were, listening in rapture to the rhythms of her breath and mine, hearing our cry of ecstasy, our soaring heartbeat, and finding ourselves lost in the tender joy of joining into one.

When she fell asleep I rose from her bed, put on my leather jacket, picked the comforter from the floor and covered her up to her ears. Then I left the room, closing the door with a soft thud behind me.

Downstairs, as I headed out of the elevator, the space looked deserted, which was a strange thing considering all the lights burning in the huge chandelier and all that glitz everywhere, as if there should have been a grand party. At the reception counter, a lone clerk with eyes glazing over leaned into his elbows, ready to nod off. The only thing that brought life into the place was the gramophone.

The same record was spinning around on it, playing,

Dark or light, I always knew
In my whole world there's no one else but you
Whether you're here or there
Baby, you're the one for whom I care
I pine for you day and night

Yours Forever I'm Going to Be

Chapter 21

Until my departure three weeks later I had little chance to
see Natasha, because of her busy schedule, which took her
away from the city and out of my reach. I stayed at Uncle
Shmeel's place, and she called me there every evening just to
chat and to tell me about her performance the night before,
which often included Beethoven's Fifth. It reminded me that I
was yet to listen to her playing it in concert.

There was so much to learn about who she was,
which I found inspiring. I was happy just to hear her
voice and said nothing, not a word about how badly I
missed her. After all I didn't want to make our
separation more difficult than it had to be.

Uncle Shmeel was quick to sense my mood. Having
left the room during my phone conversations with her,
which was his way of giving us a sense of privacy, he
would come back in later to play his clarinet for me.

Yours forever where ever I go

I'm faithful to you, never forget

From the moment we met, so long ago

Still aching for you, don't leave just yet

Say you'll return, no one knows when

But I'll keep you in my thoughts

Hold me close, kiss me again

Yours forever I'm going to be

Where ever you are just think of me

As for Natasha moving into my father's apartment, her Ma had taken care of it, with her usual manner of efficiency and with no need, thank you very much, for my help. Feeling dejected I spent my days doing little of anything, except writing.

By now I had made up my mind that my protagonist would be named not Ryan but Leonard. That was my given name in its fuller, more lionized form. In the context of my story it sounded somewhat pompous, which served a purpose: to separate the character from me, even though his feelings were loosely based on mine.

Accordingly I titled the story *Leonard and Lana*. Little did I know that this minor literary choice would later become cause for regret. It would haunt me for the rest of my life.

Missing Natasha started to weigh me down. With each passing day I felt as if the end was coming, as if I would soon lose her. On an upbeat note I used these fears, handing them over to my character, which helped flesh him out and make the story believable, giving a ring of truth to its fiction.

In spite of himself, Leonard knew he missed the rhythm of her breathing. He missed it terribly. He needed to hear the swish of her hair, the soft patter of her footfalls, and above all, the way she talked.

He wondered what Lana knew about him, having studied him so diligently from the beginning. Then he wondered if he, in turn, knew anything about her. Who she was, the inner language of her thoughts. For the first time in twelve months, he wondered if her dreams played out in a heavy Russian accent.

One morning I caught Uncle Shmeel reading my first draft. Tears welled in his eyes, which surprised me. It was the best reward I could expect, to touch another soul.

"Don't mind me," he said, wiping his face and sniffling a bit. "I'm just an old man with a soft spot at heart. Call me a romantic!"

"You're biased, Uncle Shmeel—"

"Maybe so—"

"I'm not much of a writer, but I am a hell of a catalyst."

"You, my boy, have a gift! I'm sure that others will agree with me. What you've written here awakens so many feelings, and they overwhelm me, especially now, because of my old girlfriend, Pearl."

"Why, what happened?"

"As you may recall, she's been waiting for a wedding ring for the last ten years—or maybe it was eleven, who's counting—and along the way she's been spoiling me rotten with one gift after another, simply to pave the way to the altar, until at long last she's run out of patience and left me, without any advance warning, mind you, and why? For no better reason than getting a marriage proposal from some younger fool."

I gave him a little pat on the back to show sympathy, which turned out to be the wrong thing to do, because now he started sobbing.

I stood there not knowing what to say.

Finally, in an effort to shift the conversation to practical matters, I said, "Listen, Uncle Shmeel. I'm leaving for London tomorrow. Anything I can do right now to help you around here? Just say the word!"

Between one whimper and another he pointed at the burnt-out light bulb in the kitchen.

I asked for a ladder, which he did not have.

"The other day," he said, "I climbed from the chair to the table, and I tried to reach up, which wasn't easy for me, and somehow I managed to screw it, I mean, I screwed that light bulb almost all the way in, at which time I got tired, too tired to finish the job, because really, how long can an old man keep holding his hands up in the air?"

I hopped on top of the table and tightened the thing.

"There," I said, jumping down. "It's done."

"I'm so proud of you," he said, beaming at me through the tears. "You can do anything!"

I shrugged. "It's a simple thing, Uncle Shmeel. Anyone could've done it."

"It's a question of style," he said. "You did it the same way you wrote that story."

"How so?"

"With a surprising twist at the end."

For the rest of the day he would not stop raving about my skills. His unrelenting enthusiasm flattered me and at the same time, made me uneasy. I did not think my writing deserved such praise and felt compelled to examine each paragraph, each sentence. I refined a phrase here, a phrase there, and searched for simpler, more direct words, to achieve a stronger impact.

By dawn, the story was seven pages long. I knew it was quite amateurish, but on a whim decided to send it to a literary magazine.

It was the morning of my flight. There was no time to figure out the requirements regarding the format of literary submissions. Instead of typing it double-spaced I wrote my manuscript longhand, in my usual handwriting: with minute letters and barely a space to allow any breathing.

In addition I had no idea that a stamped, self-addressed envelope should be included, so the magazine could return it to me in case it got rejected.

No doubt, the story was imperfect, but at this point, what more could I do? For lack of time I accepted the prospects of failure. I told myself that if Moses were to come down today from mount Sinai with the Ten

Commandments, he would have to spend the rest of his life trying to get them published. Compared to him, what were my chances?

Success was elusive. I dropped the manuscript at the post office and decided not to give it another thought.

Up until the very last minute I was hoping that Natasha would make it to the airport. She had promised she would. I ached to hold her in my arms, to kiss her goodbye. Counting the seconds I waited, waited, waited for her, in vain.

In later years I would learn that she did come back to New York that morning. Running through the terminal she pushed her way through the crowd, only to see the aircraft starting to pivot around the axis of its landing gear. It was still on the ground, but its nose was already being raised to effect liftoff. At first, a strong headwind reduced the ground speed, but eventually the plane managed to accelerate into a takeoff, carrying me away.

The engine was droning. Clouds started drifting over the wings and across the glass, blocking my view of the earth, falling away.

I took off my leather jacket and out of its pocket pulled out the envelope, the long, perfumed envelope Natasha had given me on our last date. In it she had sealed her diary entry, dating back to the first time we met.

Looking at the letters she had drawn on the back of the envelope—N for Natasha, combined with a fancy pen stroke with L for Lenny—I remembered promising her that I would not read it immediately, but rather save it for later.

The moment has come. I tore it open.

Unlike the letters she had sent me at the beginning of this year, here was a conversation not with me but with herself, baring her heart to the paper without any inhibitions.

She wrote,

Love at first sight?

That's a myth, an overused figure of speech, one that signifies nothing. That's what I thought, until tonight.

I never believed it could happen to me. Boy was I mistaken!

It's late at night. Mama's gone to bed, and I know she is angry with me. Tomorrow she will calm down into an outburst, which means that she'll subdue her emotions just enough to be able to give me an earful.

I can just imagine what she is going to say. "You shouldn't be changing your program on the fly, which is quite bad in itself, and even worse because you did it without consulting me. What, am I not your Mama? Have I not taken care of you, kept you safe all these years? Where's the respect? Where's the gratitude? Why didn't you say something to me ahead of time? I could have prevented you from this foolery, or at least given proper notice to the announcer, who got all confused because of you, and to the organizers, who stuck all those fliers around the auditorium to let everyone know what you were supposed to play tonight, and didn't."

To which I would say, "Sorry, Ma."

And she would go on to tell me how lucky I am to get this opportunity to play this wonderful piece, Rachmaninoff's Piano Concerto No. 3, no less, and I shouldn't have blown it, because other musicians, less fortunate than me, are listed as cooks and bakers, simply because there's no authorization for a band, at this camp and everywhere else in the military, and when they manage to play music, under such lowly job titles, all they do is march about every day beating drums and stuff, merely to accompany recruits from the train to the main part of the camp.

Then she would add that there was a chance, a slight one but all the same crucial, to meet Irving Berlin himself, as he had one of his four personal pianos delivered to Camp Upton, because of planning to write all the tunes for a musical, to be titled This is the Army. And so all in all, my performance here was vital to my career, because who knows, maybe he was sitting there, in the audience, among all those good-for-nothing low-lives in uniform, who sleep who-knows-where with God-knows-who, so in Heaven's name, the last thing we need is stunts like the one I pulled tonight.

She does not understand me, and never will.

For weeks now I cannot stop thinking of Pa and of his lost memory. I agonize over the manner of his death, because I should have done something, anything to ease it for him. I should have said goodbye or just held his hand. Instead I wasted the moment, and I can never bring it back to make it right, never. I spent it repeating over and over, hoping he would hear me, hoping desperately to be recognized, "It's me, Pa! It's Natasha!"

Ma says that grief must be held back, or else it will hinder me. She says the way to fight it is by getting back into my routine, just as I did at Juliard.

Is she right? In truth I have no idea.

Playing would be my tribute to him, she says, because it was Pa who taught me how to listen to music, how to let others hear it.

So that was my intention, to obey her. I never thought of changing my program, until it was my turn to step onstage.

It was then that I laid eyes on this soldier, this strikingly handsome man, whose shoulder was bulging out, for some reason, whose shirt looked lopsided because of it, and whose name I didn't know.

Perhaps I never will.

His smile was irresistible. It made me melt inside. I loved the way he came after me, with no hesitation whatsoever, which amazed me. I am trained from childhood to reflect on every note, consider every interpretation, and measure every feeling by the precision of an inner metronome.

He's different.

By instinct, this I know: he would complete me.

In his own way, which I found both crazy and adorable, he dashed onto the stage ahead of me, pretending to be my bugle boy, even though his instrument was made up of air.

Watching him I could set aside my anguish. In a blink, a weight was lifted off my shoulders. Oh, I could breathe! I could smile again! He brought laughter into my heart, light into my gloom.

And it was because of him—no, it was for him— that I broke the rules. On a whim I changed my plan and played something outside my regular repertoire. For him, and for all the soldiers there, some of whom may soon perish in battle, God Bless America.

And with that I gave him the best of me, the only way I knew how: through music.

At the sound of it Ma fainted.

She would never approve of him, never.

I know it.

Instead she would tell me I'm too naive and too vulnerable, and the best thing I could do is to learn to control myself.

Was she never young? Did she never feel this— this feeling that quickens my heart? It has no shape, no reason, and can be described by no other name but danger, and yet here I am, opening my arms to embrace it.

I am in awe of what is happening to me. I am scared of it and at the same time, I find myself elated.

Until Ma wakes up I have the night to myself, and it is magical.

I open the door and step out into the garden. Light rain is falling, and in each drop you can see a glint of moonlight. It is captured for an instant, and then, with a tinkle, released into a fine mist upon the dark, drenched soil.

Rising to my tiptoes I lift my hands up to the height of his shoulders. I imagine him there, in the drizzle. He's playing his invisible bugle. I can almost hear it, trembling in the wind.

Faithful forever I promise to be. I will wait for him, wait till he puts down his instrument and takes hold of me.

He will be running his fingers down, all the way down to the small of my back, touching his lips to my ear, breathing his name, breathing mine.

Here I am, dancing with air.

Around and around we go.

I Will Help You Rise

Chapter 22

O ver the years, I read this entry in her diary—the only one Natasha allowed me to read—a thousand times, and usually it puts a smile on my lips, but oh, not now, not anymore. For some reason her words have taken on a different meaning, a darker one, which I sense now for the first time, in the context of her turn for the worse.

Holding the paper makes my hands tremble. I prefer to attribute it to my age, not to anguish.

The night has been long, and long have I been waiting for her to awaken, so I can prepare her. I need to ready both of us for that head X-ray exam, which until yesterday I have been reluctant to schedule. It will, I'm afraid, result in the dreaded diagnosis which neither she nor I want to hear. But at this point, what choice do I have? Her condition can no longer be ignored. It is time to find out the name of it.

Back to that page from her diary. After three decades the ink is faded, and the paper—yellowed and crinkly. I can read it still, mostly by touching the indentations and combining what I feel with what has already been committed to memory. I close my eyes to hear her, whispering out of the papery rustle.

I am in awe of what is happening to me. I am scared of it and at the same time, I find myself elated.

Being elated is something of the past for both of us. But like the way she used to be I find myself scared and in awe. Where we're headed is yet unknown, except for one thing: her path and mine are just about to diverge.

So much has happened since the time we met, the time of our happiness. So many twists and turns during years of war and years of peace. We made promises to each other, promises that were bigger than what we could keep, which made us rise to our better selves, striving to fulfill them.

It also made for a lifelong struggle. She started out as a rising star, and I—a soldier. Her aspirations were different from mine, so we had to learn how to bridge our differences.

Some of our memories are full of joy. I bring them gently into mind. Others swoop out of nowhere to startle me.

And of all these moments, the ones that are dearest, most precious to me come from the very beginning. The first time I saw her. The first letter she wrote to me. Our first date. First kiss. The first time I made love to her.

And through it all, a great yearning.

Serving my military duty in Europe meant that for several years—from my departure in 1942 until my final return to the States in 1945, at the end of the war—

there was an ocean separating us. But I had high hopes, back then. Even in her absence she was constantly in my thoughts, and I in hers. Not so now. I care for her, but at times I sense that she doesn't even know who I am.

"I'm on your side," I murmur to her, but she turns to the wall and I am unsure if my words can reach her.

It's a new day: January 1st, 1970. The first rays of dawn break through the blinds. They stray gingerly into the room, crawl across the floor, and reach for the mattress as if in hesitation, careful not to touch her ankle, dangling from the bed, or the folds of the blanket, gathered around her chest.

Natasha is asleep by my side, her hair spread over my arm. I hold my breath, watching the shadow of her eyelashes flutter upon her cheeks. Where are her dreams taking her? She looks so beautiful, so peaceful. I have to stop myself from cuddling up to her, let alone allowing my passion to take over, because who knows what Natasha may do, thinking me a stranger.

She is not the only one confused: I am too, because even as I remind myself not to touch her, I can barely help myself. My body has a mind of its own. It compels me into arousal.

I stroke her skin, ever so tenderly, and I ache for her, because more than ever before, she is absent.

Until she opens her eyes I can make believe everything is going to be all right. Perhaps the change in her is still reversible. Perhaps there is some cure for it, or at least some treatment to stop it from worsening. It can happen this way, can't it? With a little bit of luck she may heal, and then go back to teaching piano. Her students will all come back. So will the friends who have drifted off.

Until then it's a rough time for me. I have to survive it all by myself. My son is distant, in every sense of the word. How that happened, I am yet to figure out. In my loneliness I feel so weary, so close to despair—but somehow find a way to pull myself together, simply because I must.

If I break down, what chance would she have?

To get a grip over myself I direct my thoughts elsewhere, to my craft. I think of writing about us, about this adventure called life. The few who may read it will surely complain about the story not having a happy end. Like them I wish for it. I pray with all my heart that it'll happen. But even if doesn't, here is what I have come to believe: perhaps the best anyone can hope for is to have a happy beginning.

I am grateful to have lived through so many good moments, so many memories to cherish.

Among other disappointments life dealt me was my failure to publish any of my stories—except one: *Leonard and Lana*.

Years ago Uncle Shmeel sent me a copy of the magazine where the story was printed. I wrote back to thank him and to say that it must have been beginner's luck.

Then I shared the news with Natasha, expecting her to encourage me, to root for my success as a writer, but no! To my astonishment she hated the story, perhaps because it centered on another woman, and because—to add insult to injury—the hero carried my given name. In her mind I was covering up an affair to spare her feelings, and at the same time, revealing it to the world in a fancy literary disguise. No amount of explanation could ease her suspicion, which soured the taste of our love.

Such is the power of the written word.

One time she even addressed me by the name her Ma invented for me, using the same intonation, slighting me.

"Listen here, Dostoyevsky," she said.

And I asked, "Can't you forget about that awful story?"

"Should I?"

"Please do," I pleaded. "Sorry I ever put pen to paper. Believe me, it was nothing but a scribble, an amateurish attempt at composition, which doesn't mean there was ever an affair." And thinking about my penmanship I added, "I was too young to know what I was doing."

But Natasha took it as an excuse for infidelity. "Sure!" she said, with a sudden, green flash in her eyes. "If you cannot remember it, you don't have to confess, do you."

It irked me then. But now, looking forward, this I know: a day may come when I will be happy to hear her call me by that name, because it will signal some sort of recognition.

It will give me hope.

I wish I could lie here forever, by her side, but it's time to get up. First I turn on the radio. A song is playing, and it is so beautiful, so poignant, such a fitting note to accentuate what I feel, to bring about a possible conclusion to the highs and lows of the music of us.

> In times of sorrow, when you sigh
>
> When tears well in your eyes
>
> I will kiss them dry
>
> I'm on your side
>
> You're not alone, no need to cry
>
> Between us there is no divide

> If you're in trouble, if you stumble and fall
>
> I will help you rise
>
> If you happen to falter, if you crawl
>
> I will help you rise

I put my pants on, go to the kitchen, fill a small pot with water and bring it to a boil for the eggs. Meanwhile I squeeze grapefruit juice into two glasses and wait for the two slices of bread to pop out of the toaster. I set two plates on the table, one on each side of the crystal vase. It is the same vase her Pa bought for her Mama to mark their anniversary a generation ago.

I had been too drained to think about it until last night, when on a whim I bought a bouquet of fresh flowers in lovely hues of white, pink, and purple. Why did I do it? Perhaps for old times' sake. By now I have stopped hoping to surprise my wife with such frivolities, because she pays little attention, lately, to the things I do. So for no one in particular I stand over the thing, rearranging the orchids, spray roses, and Asiatic lilies as best I can, to create an overall shape of a dome.

And then—then, in a blink—I find myself startled by a footfall behind me. A heartbeat later I hear her voice, saying, "Lenny?"

I turn around to meet her eyes. My God, this morning they are not only lucid but also shining with joy.

In a gruff voice, choked, suddenly, with tears, I ask her, "What is it, dear?"

And she says, "Don't forget."

"What, Natashinka?"

"I love you."

Spreading my arms open I stand there, speechless for a moment. Without a word she steps into them. We snuggle, my chin over her head. She presses it to my bare chest. I comb through her hair with my fingers. And once again, we are one.

Then she points at the vase.

"For you," I say. "Looks like some old painting, doesn't it?"

"Still life," she whispers. "With memories."

Then Natasha lifts her eyes, hanging them on my lips as if to demand something of me, something that has been on her mind for quite a while. Somehow I can guess it. She is anticipating an answer, which I cannot give.

Instead I kiss her. She embraces me but her eyes are troubled, and the question remains.

"Without the memories," she asks, "is it still life?"

~ The End ~

To be continued with

STILL LIFE WITH MEMORIES
VOLUME IV

The previous novels in this series:

STILL LIFE WITH MEMORIES
VOLUME I+II

About this Book

Lenny goes as far back as the moment he met Natasha during WWII, when he was a wounded warrior and she—a star, brilliant yet illusive. Natasha was a riddle to him then, and to this day, with all the changes she has gone through, she still is.

"Digging into the past, mining its moments, trying to piece them together this way and that, dusting off each memory of Natasha, of how we were, the highs and lows of the music of us, to find out where the problem may have started?"

To their son, Ben, that may seem like an exercise in futility. For Lenny, it is a necessary process of discovery, one that is as tormenting as it is delightful. He often wonders: can we ever understand, truly understand each other—soldier and musician, man and woman, one heart and another? Will we ever again dance together to the same beat? Is there a point where we may still touch?

This is a historical fiction novel about world war II wounded warrior military romance, a young woman love story. It is also one of family sagas best sellers. Do you like this genre, especially when it is tinged with family saga romance, and wrapped with a second chance in love with a strong female lead? Then this family saga series, Still Life with Memories, is for you.

About the Author

U vi Poznansky is a *USA TODAY* bestselling, award-winning author, poet and artist. "I paint with my pen," she says, "and write with my paintbrush."

Uvi earned her B. A. in Architecture and Town Planning from the Technion in Haifa, Israel. During her studies and in the years immediately following her graduation, she practiced with an innovative Architectural firm, taking part in the design of a large-scale project, *Home for the Soldier.*

Having moved to Troy, N.Y. with her husband and two children, Uvi received a Fellowship grant and a Teaching Assistantship from the Architecture department at Rensselaer Polytechnic Institute. There, she guided teams in a variety of design projects and earned her M.A. in Architecture. Then, taking a sharp turn in her education, she earned her M.S. degree in Computer Science from the University of Michigan.

During the years she spent in advancing her career—first as an architect, and later as a software engineer, software team leader, software manager and a software consultant (with an emphasis on user interface for medical instruments devices)— she wrote and painted constantly. In addition, she taught art appreciation classes.

Her versatile body of work can be seen in two websites: her blog includes thoughts about the creative process, reader reviews, author interviews, excerpts from her novels, voice clips from her audiobooks, poems and short stories. Her <u>art site</u> includes bronze and ceramic sculptures, paper engineering projects, oil and watercolor paintings, charcoal, pen and pencil drawings, and mixed media.

Coma Confidential, Overkill, Overdose, and Overdue are novels in the *Ash Suspense Thrillers with a Dash of Romance* series. With each new case, Ash uses grit and intuition to solve the crime.

Virtually Lace is the first volume in a multi-author thriller series, *High-Tech Crime Solvers*, where the authors bring each other's characters into their books.

My Own Voice, The White Piano, The Music of Us, Dancing with Air, and *Marriage before Death* are novels in the *Still Life with Memories* series, a family saga with a love story that develops in the face of hardship and illness over two generations, starting at the 1980's, then harkening back to WWII when Lenny, a soldier, and Natasha, a rising star, first met. These books are also offered in two bundles: *Apart from Love* and *Apart from War*.

Rise to Power, A Peek at Bathsheba, and *The Edge of Revolt* are novels in *The David Chronicles*, telling the story of David as you have never heard it before: from the king himself, telling the unofficial version, the one he never allowed his court scribes to recount. In his mind, history is written to praise the victorious— but at the last stretch of his illustrious life, he feels an irresistible urge to tell the truth. These books are also offered in a trilogy.

In addition, *The David Chronicles* includes six art collections: *Inspired by Art: Fighting Goliath, Inspired by Art: Fall of a Giant, Inspired by Art: Rise to Power, Inspired by Art: A Peek at Bathsheba, Inspired by Art: The Edge of Revolt,* and *Inspired by Art: The Last Concubine.*

A Favorite Son, a new-age twist on an old yarn, is inspired by the biblical story of Jacob and his mother Rebecca, plotting together against the elderly father Isaac, who is lying on his deathbed.

Twisted is a unique collection, laden with shades of mystery. Here, you will come into a dark, strange world, a hyper-reality where nearly everything is firmly rooted in the familiar—except for some quirky detail that twists the yarn.

Home and *Can We Still Love*, Uvi's deeply moving poetry books in tribute of her father, include her poetry and prose as well as translated poems from the pen of her father, the poet, author and artist Zeev Kachel.

Uvi wrote and illustrated two children's books, *Jess and Wiggle* and *Now I Am Paper*. Watch the beautiful animations she created for these books on YouTube.

About the Cover

I n designing the cover for this book I had in mind a particular passage, where Natasha is just about to perform, and her hand is raised over the keys in contemplation of the notes:

With that Natasha handed the microphone back to him and curtsied to the audience. A wavy, red strand of hair slinked from her headband, which was decorated with delicate flowers, and glided over her bare shoulder. Below that, the bodice of her dress glinted as she turned around. And again, for just a second, I thought I felt her eyes fluttering in my direction, meeting my gaze. Everyone around me must have imagined that, too.

Natasha lifted the long, silky skirt of her dress, so its folds fanned out from the seam that hugged her hips. As she sat down they draped, full and flowing, over the piano bench, responding playfully to the light from above with a cherry red shine. A reflection of it lit her chin from below and lined the underside of her slender arms, just a touch. With a slow, deliberate motion she lifted her hand, letting it hover, for what seemed like the span of a thought, over its shadow over the keys.

Her fingers started flitting across the keys, and at once I was taken by the solemn, dramatic sounds she made rise over us. They came pressing against the far reaches of the hall, gathering ominously just below the vaulted ceiling, as if in preparation to blow it away and sweep us into the night.

A Note to the Reader

Thank you for reading this book! I hope you enjoyed it. If you did, I invite you to check out more books from the same pen. There is always a new project on my drawing board, so come back to check it out.

I would love to hear what you thought of this book. You have the power of bringing it to the attention of more readers, by posting your own review. It would mean so much to me.

And another thing you can do to help me spread the word is this: please tell your friends about my work. How else will they hear about the story? How else will the characters, who sprang from my mind onto these pages, leap from there into new minds?

Bonus Excerpts
Excerpt: My Own Voice

The minute our eyes met, I knew what to do: so I stopped in the middle of what I was doing, which was dusting off the glass shield over the ice cream buckets, and stacking up waffle cones here and sugar cones there. From the counter I grabbed a bunch of paper tissues, and bent all the way down, like, to pick something from the floor. Then with a swift, discrete shove, I stuffed the tissues into one side of my bra, then the other, 'cause I truly believe in having them two scoops—if you know what I mean—roundly and firmly in place.

Having a small chest is no good: men seem to like girls with boobs that bulge out. It seems to make an awful lot of difference, especially at first sight, which you can always tell by them customers, drooling.

I straightened up real fast, and it didn't take no time for him to come in. I was still serving another customer, some obnoxious woman with, like, three chins. She couldn't make up her mind if she wanted hot fudge on top or just candy sprinkles, and what kind, what flavor would you say goes well with pistachio nut, and how about them slivered almonds, because they do seem to be such a healthy choice, now really, don't they.

He came in and stood in line, real patient, right behind her. So now I noted his eyes, which was brown, and his high forehead and the crease, the faint crease right there, in the middle of it, which reminded me all of a sudden of my pa, who left us for good when I was only five, and I never saw him again —but still, from time to time, I think about him and I miss him so.

I could feel Lenny—whose name I didn't know yet—like, staring at me. It made me hot all over. For a minute there, I could swear he was gonna to ask me how old I was—but he didn't.

And so, to avoid blushing, I turned to him and I said, boldly, "It's a crime?"

And he said, "What?"

And I said, "To be sixteen. It's a crime, you think?"

And he said, "Back in the days when I was young and handsome, that was no crime."

And I countered with, "Handsome you still are!"

He had no comeback for that, and me, I didn't have nothing with which I could follow it up. So I asked, "So? What kind of cone for you?" but that woman cut in, 'cause I was still holding her three-scoops tower of pistachio nut on a sugar cone. And she started to cry out, and like, demand some attention here, because hey, she was first in line and how about whipped cream? Or some of that shredded coconut?

So I smiled at her, in my most cool and polite manner, and squeezed out a big dollop of whipped cream, which was awesome, 'cause it calmed her down right away.

And I scattered some of them coconut flakes all over—quite a heap—and went even further, adding a cherry on top. At last, I raised the thing to my lips, because at this point, it was starting to drip already.

Then, winking at him, I passed my tongue over the top, and all around the ice cream at the rim of the cone, filling my whole mouth and, just to look sexy, also licking the tips of my fingers. Then I came around the counter, swaying my hips real pretty, and steadying myself over the wobbly high heels. I came right up to him, and before he could guess what kind of trouble I had cooked up in my head, I kissed him—so sweet and so long—on his lips, to the shouts and outcries of the offended customer.

Excerpt: Dancing with Air

Overcome, suddenly, by exhaustion, Natasha stepped out of my embrace and plopped onto her suitcase. "Ma came to say goodbye, " she said. "I saw her across from me, as we left the shore. She was offering a prayer, tears running down her cheeks. Then, once out to sea, the Germans fired at us."

"Really? What happened?"

"The ships, they took up their positions in the convoy and plodded ahead. Straightaway, two of them were lost. One ran aground. The other, suffering from engine trouble, turned back to the harbor. And as for us I thought that was the end."

I shuddered at the thought.

"This journey," said Natasha, "it was more challenging than anything I've gone through in the past. Even watching Papa during his last months was easier, in a way, because back then I was on the outside, observing his pain."

I waited for her to continue.

After a slight reflection, she added, "I could only guess what was happening to him, I mean, the ways his illness drained his mind, the ways he suffered. But now, I wasn't an observer. I lived it, Lenny! Everyone on board—including me—was going through the same fear, the same hardship."

I could not help but ask her, "What were you thinking, putting yourself at risk?"

In reply, she rose to her feet. "For this very moment," she said, clinging to me, "I would go through it all over again."

I took a step back, to stress, "Your Mama, she's beside herself with worry, and as for me—"

"You talked to her?" asked Natasha, her eyes twinkling. "Of course you did, how else would you know to wait here for me? She doesn't get it—"

"And neither do I!"

"But Lenny, it's so simple! I missed you—"

"That's no reason, Natasha, for what you've done. Why leave home, especially now, when we're at war? If you love me, keep yourself safe, if only for my sake! Why, why put your life at risk—"

"Perhaps," she said, "I'm not looking for safety! Have you ever thought of that? Perhaps something else is more important to me."

"Like what?"

"I can't continue to depend on others, Lenny, the way I've done all my life. This is my time to change, to demand new things of myself, even if they happen to frighten me, even if I'm scared out of my mind."

"Not sure I understand—"

"Please try, Lenny."

"What is it you want?"

"Just this: to stop leaning on those closest to me."

"You could've done that back home, couldn't you?"

"That's the place where I'm being taken care of, to the point of feeling stuck. Worse than that: suffocated. Someone, usually Mama, drives me to where I need to be. Someone points me to the dressing room, calls me to the stage. I'm nothing more than a mechanical doll. All I do is respond."

"You do much more than that! You excite audiences, Natasha! And to me, you're an inspiration—"

"Yes, you admire the way I play, but in truth music is the only thing for which Papa trained me."

"You're too critical of yourself," I said.

To which she said, "No, Lenny. I've seen him decline, seen him lose his mind, and if—if, like him, I'll ever lose mine—how in the world will I recover? How will I find my way, when I've never developed the skill to do so?"

I lowered my head before her.

"Never," I said, "until now."

"Exactly," said Natasha. "Until now."

And a moment later, blotting the corner of her eye, where a tear was forming, she whispered to me, "Come closer, Lenny, snuggle up, but never, ever let me lean on you."

Excerpt: Marriage before Death

Without uttering a sound I gave her a look, begging her to leave. Rochelle gave one to me, begging me to play along.

Out loud she said, "Oh how I hate you! I hate you now more than I ever loved you!"

At that, the SS officer burst out laughing. It lasted quite a while, or so it seemed to me, and by the time it finally ended, a cruel smile was left across his face, stretching from one pointy ear to the other.

"*Ach*," he hissed. "What a woman! Cold one minute—hot the next!"

Rochelle hung her eyes on me one more time.

"At the very least," she implored, "you should say you are sorry, so sorry to have left me in such a difficult situation!"

The SS officer cut in.

"Didn't I tell you?" he asked her. "His kind, they have no morals! Worse than animals is what they are."

She turned away and went back to his side. From there she said, in a tone of regret, "Right you are. I was naive, up to now, to hope for anything different from him."

Over her sorrow, the SS officer went on to say, "How could you ever let yourself be seduced by such a man?"

She shook her head. "How silly of me! How foolish it is to hope! I was sure he would confirm to everyone here his desire to marry me."

To which the SS officer said, "Now, mademoiselle, you have learned your lesson."

She gave him a tearful smile, but then could not help crying out to me, "Oh, for heaven's sake, don't you get it? I'm expecting your child!"

At that I had a change of heart. Why? First, because I was moved to tears by her plea, no matter if it was a fake one or not; and second, because what had I got to lose?

So I uttered, "Forgive me, Rochelle."

"What?" she asked. "What did you say?"

"Forgive me," I said, with a catch in my throat. "If I were a free man I would gladly keep my promise to you."

A triumphant smile played on her red lips. Yet, for just a moment, she was silent.

I thought she might make peace with me, now that I relented. Instead, she turned to the SS officer.

"Herr Müller," she said. "I'm not here to beg for mercy for this man."

In surprise, "You're not?" he asked, raising a thick eyebrow.

And from the other side of the table, his French collaborator echoed, "You're not?"

My face was still burning, still stinging from that slap of hers. I bit my lips to overcome the pain. If I could muster the nerve to speak up once more, I would ask her the very same thing.

Really? You're not?

"No," she stressed.

The toothbrush mustache under Herr Müller's nose started to twitch. Perhaps he was becoming suspicious of her.

"I thought," he said, "that you had a big favor to ask of me."

And she said, "I do."

And he said, "Well? What is it, then?"

"For the sake of my family," said Rochelle, "for the pride of my father, for my own honor, and for the future of this baby, I cannot be an unwed mother! I'd rather die!"

Becoming somewhat impatient, "*Ach!*" he said. "You should have thought of that earlier, before you got involved with the likes of him."

It was then that she said, "I promise, Herr Müller, giving me what I ask for is sure to give you the greatest pleasure, because it is just what this man deserves."

"Which is what?"

"Marriage before death."

Excerpt: The White Piano

"Stop right there," I tell him. "It makes no sense to me! Why would she want to leave you right then, at the turning point of her life, when you could be there, by her side, fighting to hold her back, away from the brink?"

"This," says my father, "is something I, too, do not understand. Up to that point Natasha has changed, quietly, and grown so much stronger than me, to the point that, no matter how hard I tried, there was no pleasing her. Then she got word, somehow, about my moment of weakness: my fling, this little, one-night thing—that was all it was, back then—with Anita."

I look at him as if to say, Who cares about your moment of weakness? So far it has lasted ten years.

He looks away, saying, "Your mom, she was mad at me. She flared up in anger. It was painful. More painful than I had expected. Was she too proud to forgive me? Did she expect me to fight harder for her, so that she may take me back someday? There was no way to know. My God, she let me feel I was done, I was no longer needed."

"But, dad," I say, "did she believe she could face it alone, whatever *it* was? Was she willing to risk everything, and for what? For no better reason than pride?"

"God," he says. "I wish I knew."

"Enough," I say. "I don't want to hear it."

"That's just the thing, Ben. Natasha kept quiet, all these years, and so did I, for her sake. Gradually, her memory problems got worse and yet, no one knew: not our friends, not even her students, because she was so afraid, afraid to lose them. Teaching, for her, became more than a livelihood: it was the last token of her independence."

"You should have told me, dad."

"Well, how could I? There was no one here to whom I could talk."

"So, since then, has mom been diagnosed?"

"Well, son, it took a long time," he says, in a tired tone of voice, "Four years after she had left me, that was when they found out, at long last. And you, Ben, you were in Europe then, off to your medical studies, or something, with a light suitcase, and a heart heavy with anger, who knows why."

I want to say, Because I had to go, to be some place else. Because I had no family, with you cheating and mom throwing her wedding ring away. That's why. But without waiting for an explanation, my father moves on to say, "I just could not do it, could not bring myself to open up, to tell you about it."

Suddenly his voice trembles, and he wraps his arms around me, which makes me unsure if this is to lean on me—or perhaps, to protect me.

"Ben," he says, "this disease, unfortunately, it can strike in the prime of life. Natasha was forty-six when, after years of knowing that something was going terribly wrong, and not being able to put a finger on it, they finally diagnosed her."

"And," I hesitate to ask, "does it have a name?"

There is a sound by the entrance door, then a knock, once, twice, three times—but neither one of us moves. There is a somber expression on his face. His gaze is locked into mine, and something passes between us which I cannot express in words.

Meanwhile, between one knock and another there is a smaller sound: the click of the clock. Under the glass crystal, the black hand moves around the dial, from one minute mark to the next. It advances with a measured beat, the beat of loss, life, fear —until at long last, my father takes a long breath, and allows himself to say, "The doctors, they call it Early onset Familial Alzheimer's disease."

Then he passes by me on his way to open the door; which gives me a moment to think of mom.

I picture her staring at the black-and-white image of her brain, not quite understanding what they are telling her.

The doctors, they point out the overall loss of brain tissue, the enlargement of the ventricles, the abnormal clusters between nerve cells, some of which are already dying, shrouded eerily by a net of frayed, twisted strands. They tell her about the shriveling of the cortex, which controls brain functions such as remembering and planning.

And that is the moment when in a flash, mom can see clearly, in all shades of gray blooming there, on that image, how it happens, how her past and her future are slowly, irreversibly being wiped away—until she is a woman, forgotten.

Books by Uviart

Coma Confidential

(Volume I of *Ash Suspense Thrillers with a Dash of Romance*)

Kindle: B07L92YHST Paperback: 978-1791691592

Overkill

(Volume II of *Ash Suspense Thrillers with a Dash of Romance*)

Kindle: B084GDK156 Paperback: 979-8644328192

Overdose

(Volume III of *Ash Suspense Thrillers with a Dash of Romance*)

Kindle: B07VP4S6PK Paperback: 978-1086703665

Overdue

(Volume IV of *Ash Suspense Thrillers with a Dash of Romance*)

Kindle: B08S724T4G Paperback: 979-8599499671

Ash Suspense Thrillers: Trilogy

(Volume I-III of *Ash Suspense Thrillers with a Dash of Romance*)

Kindle: B0893MJNSY Paperback: 979-8648269644

Virtually Lace

(Volume I of *High-Tech Crime Solvers*)

Kindle: B07L968RXD Paperback: 978-1790407187

My Own Voice

(Volume I of *Still Life with Memories*)

Kindle: B013TA3FBS Paperback: 978-0984993215

The White Piano

(Volume II of *Still Life with Memories*)

Kindle: B013TAU7L4 Paperback: 978-1517049447

The Music of Us

(Volume III of *Still Life with Memories*)

Kindle: B013TCYWHC Paperback: 978-0-9849932-9-1

Dancing with Air

(Volume IV of *Still Life with Memories*)

Kindle: B01I4ENROY Paperback: 978-1536896534

Marriage before Death

(Volume V of *Still Life with Memories*)

Kindle: B0746NW5CD Paperback: 978-1974001736

Apart from Love

(*Still Life with Memories Bundle I*)

Kindle: B006WPITP0 Paperback: 978-0-9849932-0-8

Apart from War

(*Still Life with Memories Bundle II*)

Kindle: B07MMZLD7Z Paperback: 978-1792131592

Rise to Power

(Volume I of *The David Chronicles*)

Kindle: B00H6PMZ0U Paperback: 978-0-9849932-4-6

A Peek at Bathsheba

(Volume II of *The David Chronicles*)

Kindle: B00LEPPDV6 Paperback: 978-0-9849932-7-7

The Edge of Revolt

(Volume III of *The David Chronicles*)

Kindle: B00Q5WVKA6 Paperback: 978-0984993284

The David Chronicles: Trilogy

(Volume I-III of *The David Chronicles*)

Kindle: B00QYGF6WG Paperback: 978-1797440699

The David Chronicles: Art

(Volume IV-XI of *The David Chronicles*)

Kindle: B08YWSH7HC Paperback: 979-8721612886

Inspired by Art: Fighting Goliath

(Art book. Volume IV of *The David Chronicles*)

Kindle: B01MSBNSE4   Paperback 978-1797726212

Inspired by Art: Fall of a Giant

(Art book. Volume V of *The David Chronicles*)

Kindle: B01MSBS82Q   Paperback: 978-1092307765

Inspired by Art: Rise to Power

(Art book. Volume VI of *The David Chronicles*)

Kindle: B01N2786VX   Paperback: 978-1092263207

Inspired by Art: A Peek at Bathsheba

(Art book. Volume VII of *The David Chronicles*)

Kindle: B01MUFS9OA   Paperback: 978-1092306225

Inspired by Art: The Edge of Revolt

(Art book. Volume VIII of *The David Chronicles*)

Kindle: B01N6ZG0W8   Paperback: 978-1091306158

Inspired by Art: The Last Concubine

(Art book. Volume IX of *The David Chronicles*)

Kindle: B01N2AXQP2   Paperback: 978-1092302715

A Favorite Son

Kindle: B00AUZ3LGU Paperback: 978-0-9849932-5-3

Twisted

Kindle: B00D7Q3IY4

Paperback: 978-0984993260 Nook: 2940151689588

Home

Kindle: B00960TE3Y

Paperback: 978-09849932-3-9 Nook: 2940151729468

Can We Still Love

(Poetry)

Kindle: B0GV3G23V4 Paperback: B0GY8Q1Y9Z

Virtually Yummy: Recipes that Inspire

(Cookbook)

Kindle: B085BDNDM5 Nook: 2940163988655

Apple: id1501182051 Kobo: 9781393589853

בית

(Poetry in Hebrew)
Paperback: 978-1494920968 Nook: 1127367962
Apple: id1302908918 Kobo: 9781540199966

Jess and Wiggle

Kindle: B013D1W0SM Paperback: 978-1494920968

Now I Am Paper

Kindle: B00YQS4O72 Paperback: 978-1494919429

www.ingramcontent.com/pod-product-compliance
Lightning Source LLC
Chambersburg PA
CBHW032032240626
47154CB00003B/871